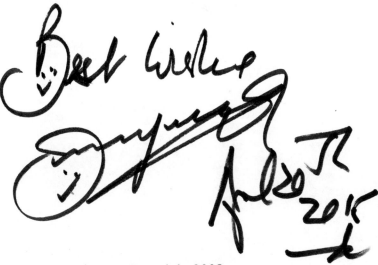

to: Nicholas

The Violin Man's Legacy

Best wishes

ISBN 9'

GW00708303

أ: الذلل محمد

إسماعيل كبلو

THE VIOLIN MAN'S LEGACY

By Seumas Gallacher

CHAPTER 1

Ang Chu was good. He knew that. Killings were the least difficult of all the initiations expected of a good man and being an enforcer for the triads marked a step up the ladder. He'd served the customary five years as a soldier in the mob, running the streets, making the savage slums combat a way of life. Two years later, the pickings on the side from the collections of enforced protection money helped to feed his growing drug habit. Chasing the dragons became easier with money to pay the beast supplier. The handover to the Mainland mandarins remained a few years away yet in 1997, but until then a lot of triad harvesting would have to be done.

Tonight was a milestone. A summons to meet with the big boss. The top guy. A high honour indeed. From here on, richer living beckoned. This night he would become a lieutenant. A triad to reckon with.

The warehouse backed on to the dockside by Kowloon harbour. He paid off the taxi two streets away and walked the rest as always. Care in everything, caution the watchword. The constant bustle and din of boat traffic on the waterways in Hong Kong made silence a non-existent concept.

A sliver of yellowing light sneaked from underneath the large, dirty, wooden doors. The noise of a slat rattling across the inside of the door-frame followed his coded rap.

A tattooed arm held one lopsided piece of the door ajar for him as he stepped from the dark into the marginally lighter gloom of the godown.

He counted around a dozen triads, some of whom he knew from the streets, others he recognized as higher-ranking gang members. At the rear of the warehouse three men sat behind a large wooden work-table. The one in the middle looked up at Ang Chu and beckoned him forward. The big man. The boss.

The half-moon birthmark on the supremo's forehead was barely visible. The magnificent adrenaline surge was even better than he got from the Grade A stuff he was using lately. No seats cluttered this side of the table. Nobody ever sat down in front of the boss. Nobody ever expected to. Chu moved forward with two men on either side of him. He bowed his head in salute, as did his companions.

Despite himself, he felt his body shake a little. He hoped they wouldn't notice. It was kind of dark anyway, so no worries. What a night.

The boss addressed him. "Ang Chu. I bid you warm welcome to our meeting. I've heard much about you."

Chu bowed again, no conversation expected unless prompted.

"Tonight is a special occasion for you and for us. Your friends here have reported fully to me on your activities. I'm a great believer that all action deserves its due reward.

Please step forward and place your hands flat upon the table in front of me."

Now for the ritual. Now for the glorious moment. Chu did as instructed. His hands flattened in supplication before the boss. The shaking had gone.

On either side of him, one man each took hold of an arm. Two others stepped forward swiftly and acted in concert. Two meat cleavers flashed and thudded through the flesh of both arms, imbedding in the solid wood beneath his fingers. The speed of their movement beat the signal of pain to his brain. His limbs severed at the wrists, he opened his mouth to cry out but the blackness engulfed him before the scream could begin.

As the dying triad was folded into the tarpaulin, the man in the middle seat spoke.

"Please remove this scum and park it with the fishes. Show the hands that stole my money around the streets to the rest of our people." His voice was quiet. "Remind them how much I value their honesty."

CHAPTER 2

Roddie Bell had been a highly efficient SAS commando in his day. Ugly situations and fire-fights featured regularly in his years of duty and all handled with exemplary professionalism. After his retirement, it didn't take long for offers to surface from the private sector. The security company, Securimax, beat off several competitors to secure his services as Chief of Operations at their European hub in Rotterdam.

The warehouse situated down near the seaport, close to all the major shipping clients. Activity started around five-thirty each morning. Roddie always clocked-in first on site, believing the best way to run a team was to lead from the front, be involved, not be scared to get his hands dirty with the rest of them.

The half-light of dawn yielded to a grey overcast day. The early shift prepared to load a shipment of gold bullion for ABN AMRO Bank in Rotterdam. Bound for the centre of the city, not too far a trip from the warehouse, the bars waited on the rolling, wooden pallet next to the security truck. Wrapped in the usual black plastic containers, the gold itself wasn't showing.

They opened the armoured vehicles doors, ready to receive the forklift's load and all hell broke loose. A gang of six players wielding AK 47s appeared, the element of surprise total. Two shots were fired into the ceiling.

"Lie down! Lie down!" screamed one of the attackers. The loaders instantly did as ordered. Roddie Bell heard the shouts and his instinctive reaction kicked in to overdrive. He sprinted towards the on-going heist, drawing the gun from his side holster. He hardly had a chance to get it out. Two of the gunmen blasted at him, ripping out his throat and lower stomach. He was dead before his body hit the stone floor.

A dark van backed up to the warehouse door and transferred the bars in just over a minute. The attackers knew what they were after. It was clear any movement from the loaders would invite the same deadly result inflicted on Bell. In the dim light a second van waited a few metres away with its engine running, the exact colouring difficult to identify. More shots fired into the roof to keep heads down. Then the gunmen disappeared. The action took less than three and a half minutes.

Value taken a touch over four point two million dollars.

CHAPTER 3

Jack Calder wasn't a guy who got drunk easily.

He and Malky McGuire had been shooting the breeze in The Crushed Grapes bar since just after opening time a couple of hours earlier. They'd been hammering the Glen Grant. Jack wasn't sober but he wasn't really drunk either. His head and the cloying, sour feeling in his throat told him he'd drunk a lot but not enough to get him to the point he wanted. Close to going home time, the noise from the few tables around them became a dull buzz.

Malky and he were frequent customers. The Crushed Grapes is a regular watering hole for middle-level executive spenders. Public relations managers, store-merchandise buyers, and neighbouring restaurant owners mingled at its tables. No art-deco trappings. No fancy furniture from the pages of the fashion magazines. A small finger-food menu meant no expensive kitchen to maintain. Drinks prices ranged higher than most of the competing bars in the area and whether intended or not, this filtered out the undesirable younger set. Trendiness stretched merely to a good sound system never turned up to a level to drown out conversation, with music such as The Commodores' 'Three Times a Lady' playing now, more likely than rock numbers.

The London offices of International Security Partners Limited situated a couple of streets from the bar. For the past ten years, Jack and Malky had shared the operational load for the specialised security services company. In their highly-focused arena, success measured more not by what happened but by what they prevented from happening. The pair ranked among the best teams in the business. No clients taken down by aggrieved competitors. No overt losses. A stream of repeat engagements. ISP had become a known and respected abbreviation in the security industry.

ISP was the brain-child of their former SAS commanding officer, Major Julian 'Jules' Townsend. He'd demobbed from the service a couple of years before them. By the time Jules asked them to join him, ISP was already established with a select clientele across Europe and he needed reliable, intelligent operatives to sustain its growth. In the late eighties and early nineties, well-paying opportunities for demobilizing elite professional soldiers were few. The money Townsend put on the table exceeded anything they could have earned elsewhere. They accepted the offer and their roles without blinking an eye. Jules trusted them as he had in the murky times in Northern Ireland and other, darker spots, where often only intuition kept a man and his sidekicks alive.

The brotherhood of fighting commandos survived long after demobilization. That morning, word flashed across the invisible security grapevine their former buddy, Roddie Bell, had died, murdered during a heist in Rotterdam. Jack and Malky were having their own private wake, as many others would do when they heard the news. The funeral would be a more public ceremony in a few days time.

CHAPTER 4

The armed robbery and killing of Roddie Bell in Rotterdam was the first of its kind in Holland in over twenty years. A few days later a second, seemingly unrelated strike shocked the country.

Guardwell Inc, a top name security company, had carried valuable cargo for more than three decades throughout Holland and neighbouring countries. A shipment of diamonds to the cutting firm of Grussweld Inc in Utrecht was a standard run.

The armoured van drew up opposite the firm's offices and parked across from a wide plaza fronting the main entrance to the building. The driver, the courier - with the gems shipment chained to his wrist - an accompanying escort from the diamond company, and a Guardwell security officer occupied the van.

The doors opened and the escort alighted, followed closely by the courier and security man together. The plaza was clear for the full thirty yards or so to the entrance, until, from nowhere, five men, clad in black, wearing Halloween-style masks, charged at the detail. Four of them brandished automatic weapons which the Guardwell man later identified as Uzi sub-machine guns. The mule's escort tried to turn back only to be hit by a burst from the leading attacker. The courier stepped forward to help him. The second round of bullets brought him down. Both men died instantly.

Faced with four weapons, the security guard lay down on the pavement as commanded. The fifth assailant moved to the dead courier with a set of bolt cutters, cutting from the man's wrist the chain securing the attache case containing the diamonds. Several bursts from the machine guns, fired into the air, made sure everyone kept their heads down.

As the raid progressed, five motor-cycles arrived together, the riders also dressed in black and masked. Each of the robbers took a pillion seat and in seconds sped off in different directions.

Three million dollars worth of gems and two lives taken in less than one minute. Very precise. Very organized. Very fast.

CHAPTER 5

The entire week, the sun struggled to fight its way through a perpetually clouded sky. A drab and grey day greeted the Thursday service.

Saint Margaret the Blessed replicated hundreds of similar stone structures around the countryside, neither ugly nor something to catch the eye or invite a casual visitor. Local pride in the church maintained the grounds which boasted neatly trimmed grass and borders of flowers.

Jack counted no more than a couple of dozen people inside. They grouped in bunches in the front two pews and at the rear. Annie Bell sat in the middle of the first line of seats across the aisle from where Jack accompanied Malky and Jules. By tacit mutual desire, no words were exchanged. A clutch of what appeared to be local family friends and four or five other former SAS guys made up the congregation.

Jack stared at the white coffin sitting astride the centre aisle where the minister stood, the book of service already opened in his hand. Several bouquets of flowers adorned the casket. Jack caught the strong floral scent as he took his place. The only other sensation he registered was in response to the solemnity of the organ music. It just seemed loud. Not sad - loud. *God, I hate this stuff.* He tried to stifle an involuntary shudder.

The grey, stone walls of the church amplified the stentorian voice of the minister as he led them through the service. For an older man, his tone resonated, not much in the way of eulogy, more a lament for "such a vital spirit, taken from us all too early."

Jack heard him speak and realized he hadn't been listening to him. The ex-soldier had attended dozens of funeral services in the course of a decade in the SAS. After a few of these, the words rarely ever captured the depth of human loss, each service special to only a handful of those present at any of them. Right now, Jack felt nothing. He wanted this over with as soon as possible.

The time came for the casket to be moved outside. Jules led Jack and Malky forward as pallbearers with another youngish-looking man. Jack recognized him as Roddie's brother, but he couldn't remember his name. Together they paced as military men do, precisely, neither slowly nor quickly, to the graveside. The formalities continued until finally the funeral director moved forward with the workmen and their spades. More words. More noises. *God, let this get finished.* The mounds of pre-dug earth piled on either side of the grave, wet and muddied.

The sound of the clods thudding on to the wood caused Jack to glance up and around him. A short distance away Annie Bell stood beside her daughter, neither of them talking. Then he caught it. It was on the widow's face. It was in the eyes. In the set of the mouth. In the cast of the head. He recalled vividly where he'd seen the look before. And memories of the Violin Man came flooding back. And another reminder why he detested funerals.

* * * * *

Tommy Calder knew nothing but life in the Glasgow slum area of Govan.

He grew up as one of seven sisters and brothers, all of whom attended basic school only until they could legitimately leave and find some sort of work to contribute to the family income.

His father was a long-serving cooper at the Fairfields shipyard on Clydeside. In line with many other fathers, he managed to install Tommy and his three brothers as apprentices in the craft guilds. Money was tight, but at least there was always a meal on the table.

Govan was a rough and ready dockside neighbourhood, forged in the shadows of the heavy industries associated with the shipyards. Life was uncompromising. A mix of Scots lowlanders and Irish immigrants bred a harsh reality. A man worked or his family went without food, any quality of life a direct result of holding down a regular job.

Entertainment was home grown. The Calder men played football on the common park green in teams of up to twenty or thirty a side, often for long hours, even when the summer evening light faded past ten o'clock.

Sometimes on weekends and holidays families arranged communal outside parties and dances, commandeering the street, with chairs placed at either end to close off what little motor traffic may have dared to intrude. Whoever owned an instrument was absorbed into an assortment of music providers, the main centre-piece usually an accordion player.

At one of these street dances, Tommy, by now in his mid-twenties, met Jenny Cafferty after an awkward introduction from one of her brothers. For all the rough and ready masculinity Tommy represented, being at ease with womenfolk didn't count as part of the deal. Jenny liked the look of the gauche Tommy Calder, and soon had him relaxed enough to get up and try a few dance steps. To his amazement, he found he enjoyed dancing. By the time the night ended they were planning when to meet again.

Four months later, their friendship had blossomed into a true depth of caring for each other.

After another month or so, Jenny tearfully confided to Tommy she was pregnant, which came as a shock to both of them. The course of action was clear to Tommy. With no thought of ducking the issue, he told Jenny's parents if her father would accept him as a son-in-law, he would be proud to husband their daughter.

After some tough talking, both families came to terms with the situation, blessed the union and began planning for the marriage a month ahead. Jack Calder was born five months later, a big baby with beautiful eyes and lungs like a foghorn, but with a smile to melt the moon. A small one-bedroom unit in a tenement building became home. Within three years Jack had as many siblings, all sisters, sharing the family pushchair. For the Calder brood, like thousands of such families in the neighbourhood, money was always scarce, but Jack recalled there was always a warm bed, food and clothing. Somewhere along the way, Tommy acquired a second-hand gramophone record player from a pal in the shipyard. Whenever he could scrape together a little spare money, he started buying long-playing records. Soon, a strange assortment of music filled the cramped Calder household most evenings, often far beyond midnight. Dance-band music and noted crooners and ballad singers of the time topped the favourites. The man from the shipyards disliked the modern style of rock and roll or country and western productions.

Perhaps the oddest part of the collection was a long-playing record of the violin prodigy, Yehudi Menuhin, playing Beethoven's Violin Concerto. Tommy told his family Menuhin was the greatest violin player the world had ever heard. No one thought to ask him how many other violin players he had actually listened to, but the sounds scraping from the old gramophone were hauntingly beautiful. The grace of Menuhin's music enveloped the small slum and Tommy seemed to drift away on the air with it. Jack remembered clearly often being told to listen. At five and six years of age he couldn't fathom why his father needed him to listen, but listen he did.

The nickname, 'Violin Man' stuck to Jack's father. Nobody ridiculed the man from the shipyards for the escape valve the violin music provided. Lord knows, they all needed something.

The turning point for the Calder family came when Tommy lost his job. Austerity hammered Scotland's big cities and he joined hundreds of his workmates whose pay-packets no longer salved a tough week. Making ends meet became increasingly difficult. With money even scarcer, Jenny held down as many as three different cleaning jobs at one time. Tommy picked up what little work was available in the slums for men desperate to keep themselves and their families alive. Lots of crying from his sisters, caused by hunger, haunted young Jack. Tommy's dogged determination to keep things going faded as the months passed. Casual jobs became scarcer and the unemployment queues longer. Frequent fist-fights erupted among the contenders for the scarce amount of work available. Jack's father was well able to look after himself physically but he began to grow desperate on the days with no work. No work meant no money. No money meant no food.

The savage, black dog of idle days without earnings or even the hope of earnings bit deeper and the debt collectors' knockings became more frequent and more hostile. Not-so-veiled threats accompanied those demands for payments of some sort. Piece by piece, the Calder family items of even limited value found their way into the pawnshops around Govan.

Periodically, Tommy would get a couple of days' relief in the form of part-time use of his physical labour.

The fact his kids might go without food clawed at him. He himself ate sparingly whenever there was something on the table in order that his family would eat. Slowly, he was drawn towards the trap of many in the same stretched hellish circumstances. Cheap wine secreted in brown paper bags from the bottle shops provided temporary solace from the frequent rounds of depression.Jenny aged in front of his eyes with the burden of spinning the timing of her work with nursing the kids. At first, Tommy became the house-husband, but as he spent more time out looking for jobs, this lapsed as his primary concern. Daily fights with Jenny became a source of mutual agitation. The smell of the cheap wine incensed her more than his inability to find work.

Tommy found a few weeks' employment bagging flour for a local tradesman. The flour was transported in bulk and delivered through a street-level trapdoor to a cellar in an old tenement building about half an hour's walk from the Calder home. Dirty, messy work, it paid barely enough to justify the labour, but better than nothing at all.

Six days a week in the dimly-lit cellar, Tommy kept the company of mice and rats scurrying around his feet. The flour clouds as he packed the half-hundredweight canvas bags permeated his clothing, finding its way into his hair, his eyes, the soles of his shoes. He detested the work.

On a cold rainy Saturday in October, Jenny persuaded her husband to take young Jack with him to get the boy out from under her nose for the day. Jack had never been there with his dad. The seven-year old thought it a marvellous adventure, going to his Daddy's work. He didn't notice the cellar was dingy. The scrabbling and squeaks from the mice held no danger for him. Oblivious to the grunts and groaning as his father filled the rough sacks with the clotting flour, this was a wonderful playground.

In between bagging, Tommy sipped from the brown paper bag, and when he talked to Jack his voice began to waver. Too young to notice any change in the demeanour of his father, he continued to trace drawings in the flour soot covering the floor of the cellar.

"Come here, wee Jack," he beckoned to the boy, as he swayed on the stool next to the bagging bench.

"Yes, Daddy. What is it?"

Tommy dug some coins from his stained jacket pocket and offered them to his son.

"Here, take these."

Jack took the money and his father drew him close in a hug and kissed him. The boy was aware of the strange smell he always smelled when his Daddy got quiet, and a lot of times when he and Mammy fought and shouted at each other.

"You know your Daddy loves you, don't you, eh? Go down to Collins' shop at the end of the road, and buy us a couple of ice-creams. You'd like that, eh?"

"Aye, Daddy."

"Take your time. You don't want them cones to fall and get ate by some doggie, do you?"

"Right. Walk back slow it is, Daddy."

"You're a good boy, wee Jack. Now listen, there's something I want you to do."

"What's that?"

"I need you to tell your Mammy, Daddy says, 'The Violin Man's stopped playin', and he's nae comin' back.' Can you remember that?"

"I think so, Daddy."

"Good boy. Now off you go and get these ice-creams before the shop shuts."

Collins' was right at the end of the road, about ten minutes walk. Jack did as his father instructed and walked back slowly. No big doggie was going to have his ice-creams.

The ice cream started to melt and dribble down his clutching hands as he got back to the building.

"I'm here Daddy," he called as he climbed down the brick stairway into the cellar.

His father didn't reply. In the half-light, he saw him lying down beside the stool, as if asleep. The dim light from the bare bulb hanging above the bench couldn't hide the stare from his Daddy's eyes. A dark pool seeped into the soiled floor, curdling the caked flour on the stone with deep-red liquid still flowing from his father's arms. Near the side of his face lay a bloodied razor blade, which had painlessly opened the arteries on his wrists.

Jack tried to guess what kind of game Daddy was playing this time, like Cowboys and Indians at school, when you try to stay still as long as you can before somebody touches you and says *Tag*, and you get to be alive again.

The Violin Man was incapable of hearing his boy trying to *Tag* him alive, but Jack Calder became equally incapable of ever erasing the death of his father from his memory.

* * * * *

The Methodist Church in Greenfield Street in Govan was a magnet for all denominations of believers. Young Jack had been a part of the youth Life Boys group since four years old, with regular Sunday School attendance a must imposed by his Mammy. He enjoyed the Sunday School children's songs, when he and his pals could really just make as much noise as they liked bringing 'Jesus close to the fishers of men' at the top of their lungs.

It rained stair-rods on the day they buried Tommy Calder. The packed church held neighbours from the streets around. A lot of snuffling into handkerchiefs. Lots of people whispering to Mammy. Some passing envelopes to his mother.

What was in them? Jack wondered.

The crowd sang 'Abide With Me' with a deafening noise. Then, silence, a few murmured voices. Big men carried the large, wooden box outside and one of his aunties moved Jack toward the door. He looked back at his Mammy standing with a group of women from their own street. One of them held Mammy's hands and stared into her face, neither of them talking. He remembered the bewilderment on his Mammy's face. Empty. Lost. Not hearing or seeing anything around her. It would take him until many years later to understand what the look meant. The Violin Man was not coming back.

* * * * *

Annie Bell's face bore the same pain as they lowered her husband into his final resting place.

He hated funerals.

* * * * *

The Reverend Thornton had officiated at hundreds of funeral services. Adept at consoling those in grief, with all the delicacy of a natural carer, he handed the widow gently into her car. He then approached Jack, about to speak. Jack spoke first. "Thank you for everything today, Reverend. We're most grateful to you. And thanks for looking after Mrs Bell so well. We all appreciate your kindness."

"Mr Calder. Each of us is touched in different ways by the passing of our nearest and dearest. Sometimes sooner. Sometimes later. May the Grace of God be with you. I'll pray for all of you tonight, including for the soul of your friend."

"Thank you," replied Jack and moved away toward Jules and Malky.

"You wanna join us for a drink, Jack?" asked the Irishman. "It's kinda early, but what the hell?"

"No thanks, Malky. If you don't mind, I'd rather go back to the flat and chill out. You know these funerals fuck with my head."

"Sure, big man. Jules and me's got stuff to catch up on. See ye later."

The emptiness numbed his thinking. The journey back to his pad in St John's Wood hardly registered.

* * * * *

The mirror told its own story. Jack's military training had spilled over into a regular exercise habit after leaving the forces, fleshing out well his six-foot-two frame. The pale-blue Scottish eyes and fair, brown hair did nothing to detract from his good looks. He wasn't a ladies man inasmuch as he didn't go searching for them. He'd had plenty of female admirers, captivated not least with the mild burr in his accent. The mirror only told part of the story. Other things preyed on his mind every now and then, things he had never learned how to handle, except by pouring himself a temporary solution from a whisky bottle. The Scotch hit the spot, good stuff - excellent malt. About half the bottle had gone and Jack *was* getting tipsy now.

What the hell, he'd buried yet another of his former buddies today hadn't he? Hadn't he? It caught him by surprise. Sneaked up on him. His neck grew cold. He shivered. Damn. Then, from his stomach, from his guts, somewhere deep inside his body even he couldn't grasp, it came.

He couldn't breathe. He gasped. He gasped again, trying for breath. Then a huge heaving wrench in his lungs. Like a drowning man searching for the first intake of air coming up from under the water. It broke as a massive sobbing noise. Then again. And again. Now he was on his knees on the carpet, his hands outstretched in front of him. He cried. He cried like he'd cried so many times before. In private. Alone. Gut-wrenching sobbing. God, it hurt.

That was only the physical part.

He realized for the umpteenth time. This was grieving. Painful grieving.

The thing was, he really didn't know if he was grieving for the death of his mate. Or grieving for the death of his father. Or grieving for the death of something in his own soul.

CHAPTER 6

In the past month, Jules Townsend had shuttled from London to Holland twice a week, pursuing the growing business between the Dutch client base and their own network in London. On the day after Roddie's burial, he, Malky and Jack played catch-up in the ISP office.

The news of the hits in Rotterdam and Utrecht made screaming headlines in the industry. Respected major security firms with prestige clients losing hefty value shipments of gold bullion and diamonds, each within a few days, was a rarity.

"It's been a bad week for everyone over there," said Jules.

"This second hit was on Gemtec," he continued. "Big players in the gems business, mostly South African diamonds, headquartered in Amsterdam. They lost a shipment in Utrecht, two of their people gunned down, cold-blooded, in the middle of the street in plain daylight. I met with Deryk Ostman, Gemtec's owner and we also talked for a long time yesterday on the phone. The police are on the case already but he wants us to do a comprehensive review of his group's security operations."

Jules removed a sheaf of Gemtec's corporate brochures from his files and passed them across to Jack.

"Go meet Ostman in Amsterdam. I reckon your fresh eye on their security protocols is what's needed. Their business is worth a lot to us if you can tie it down. Your tickets and hotel bookings are with your office as we speak. I want you on a plane tonight and to stay until you get us a result."

Jules was in the kind of mood they knew from many times on active patrol. Very intense. Very focused. "Malky, you keep running this side of the water for us, and you can have your buddy back in a month or so. If we don't have the Gemtec account by then, we never will." Nobody ever argued with Julian Townsend. The saying about him had always been, 'What the Major wants, the Major gets.'

Jack shrugged his shoulders. "You got anything else on them? I like to do my homework before I go visiting." Jules removed a second, bound folder and handed it across the table. "These are dossiers on some of their people. The Head of Security's an old acquaintance. Hubert Meiss."

Jack recalled Meiss. They'd worked more than once before with inter-jurisdictional forces in the Balkans and elsewhere, including Africa.

"Interesting," he replied, placing the brochures and the added material into his briefcase. "I'll bone up on this on the flight tonight."

* * * * *

A familiar stamping ground for all of them, Jack operated as comfortably in Amsterdam as in London. The morning after landing at Schiphol Airport, he was shown into the office of Deryk Ostman. He was the third-generation owner of Gemtec, one of the largest wholesale diamond traders in Holland. Seated to the side of Ostman was Hubert Meiss.

The dossier had provided a refresher on Meiss. Originally from Munich, stockily built, a good operator with a track record to match the best, he was ten years older than Jack. It looked to the Scotsman that the softer life away from the mercenary beat had added a few pounds around the waist. The face had lost some of the leanness of the field craftsman the SAS had worked alongside in Africa twelve years before. The riveting look from the penetrative, blue eyes had also mellowed a little. Life as chief of Gemtec security suited Meiss. The recent loss of corporate colleagues however, seemed to weigh him down. The customary stiff-necked bearing was missing. In its place a distinct sagging at the shoulders spoke volumes.

"Jack, good to see you again," Meiss began, with a firm handshake. "It's been a while, partner. This is Deryk Ostman, whom I think you know already?"

"Hi, Hubert, same here, my friend. Mr Ostman, of course I know of you but I believe this is the first time we've met. My pleasure, sir," said Jack, nodding towards the Dutchman.

"Thank you, Mr Calder. Hubert here speaks very highly of you and of ISP. Given this week's unfortunate events, I've proposed we seek the assistance of an independent agency such as yourselves to help us to understand how this tragedy happened." The gems boss also carried his grief heavily. "You're aware, of course, two of our employees were shot dead in the robbery. I can assure you that takes a higher priority at Gemtec than losing the diamond shipment. Diamonds are insurable and therefore replaceable. The lives of my personnel are not. I want you to find out *who* did this and how. My entire organization will be open to you to make whatever enquiries you feel necessary," he added, signalling to Meiss. "I've already instructed Hubert to ensure all files, records, logs and any other relevant documents be made available to you. You can work with and through Hubert, but progress reports will be directly to myself. Is that acceptable?"

Jack acknowledged the instruction. "Perfect, Mr Ostman. I understand Jules Townsend agreed with you the terms of engagement, extending for up to three months from today's date?"

"Correct. Mr Calder, my family has operated for more than seventy years in this business. Of course we've had losses in the past, but nothing worse than modest disappearances of a few stones. In every case, we've been able to identify the people involved, or at least close the process lapses in order to avoid similar things happening to us again." He leaned forward. "But, Mr Calder, we've never, repeat never, had fatalities. I have no words to describe how agonizing that is to me personally. I know the wives of those who lost their husbands, and of course we'll look after them financially. It's imperative we bring the killers to account. Whatever it takes, I'm prepared to support. Do you understand me, Mr Calder?"

Jack responded, "Yes, sir, I do understand you. I'll make you no promises which I can't guarantee at this time, other than to commit you'll get our best efforts on this."

"Thank you, Mr Calder."

Jack guessed Deryk Ostman had never faced real violence before. To Jack and his former SAS colleagues, violence represented a natural means to an end, confronting it part of the end-game.

He wondered how far Ostman was prepared to go to 'bring the killers to account.' Did he mean in a simple legal manner? Or in a more absolute sense? Time would tell. First things first. Finding out the 'how' and the 'who'.

Jack turned to Meiss. "Hubert, what've you lined up for us this morning? I'd like to start as soon as possible. The longer these things are left, the more difficult it is to get to the answers."

Meiss tapped the papers in his hand. "We're working with the heads of the Serious Crime Squads both in Utrecht and here in Amsterdam. They've been informed we're bringing you guys in on a private basis. As you might expect, some of them aren't overjoyed at the prospect, but I understand Jules is an old buddy of their Chief of Police in Amsterdam, Jens Kluvin. Jens has given the nod to let you do what you need to do. I know you won't rub them up the wrong way."

Jack smiled his appreciation. "Who's handling the documentation and papers at Gemtec?"

"My number two, Nils Bergman. He buddied with me in Honduras and South America. He joined the company about four years ago. Norwegian. Steady man. Excellent administrative mind. He'll be the key point man for document flows. He's located two floors down. Let's go introduce you."

Jack stood up "Sounds fine," he said, and turned to the boss. "Mr Ostman. Good day, sir. I'll be in touch regularly and trust we'll get this sorted out as soon as possible."

"Goodbye, Mr Calder," replied the Dutchman, without looking up from his desk.

CHAPTER 7

The career of a journeyman mercenary isn't plotted on schoolbooks.

Soldiers gravitate towards the life by accident or economic circumstance rather than by choice. Nils Bergman grew up in a small village in the countryside in the east of Norway. He saw some service and limited travel aboard a vessel in the Norwegian Merchant Navy. This he found boring, but not enough to deter him from continued involvement in military activity. He answered an advertisement for soldiers of fortune deployed in the backwaters of South America. His leader in that venture was Hubert Meiss. From Meiss, he learned the techniques of cold-hearted, guerrilla warfare tactics. Over the course of almost twenty years together, they served several paymasters in jungles and crooked third-world regions.

Jack had never met the Norwegian and the slight build surprised him, with features drawn across a tight-skinned face and balding skull. When he came forward to offer his handshake, Jack noticed a distinct limp in the left leg. Probably a bullet or shrapnel wound, he guessed. The hands matched those of a much older man.

Meiss made the introductions. "Nils and I served on and off together for more than eighteen years in South America and Africa."

That explains it, thought Jack. Looking after his buddy after he copped one in the field. Brain still good enough to get the paperwork organized.

Meiss laid out the ground rules with Jack and Bergman.

"Nils'll run you through the stuff we've shared with the Crime Squad detectives. Nils, anything Jack wants to read is cleared with Ostman. Carte blanche. He can take away copies of documents he needs, but the originals stay here. For good order's sake, log everything."

"No problem," replied Nils. "I've got it sorted in bunches on the campaign table over there by the wall. We can make a start on it now."

"Good. Okay, Jack. I'll leave you with Nils. Call me if you need anything else."

* * * * *

Everything on the table was stacked in systematic, neat piles of paper. Bergman's precision led Jack to surmise he'd been an excellent deputy to Meiss in the field, and no less so here at Gemtec.

"Where do you want to start?" Bergman asked.

"We've had detailed accounts of the hit itself," Jack answered. It would be helpful to get your take on tracing the movement of the diamonds from the source up until the killings."

For the rest of the day, Bergman talked Jack through the sequence of events as they occurred on the day of the heist. He stopped frequently to indicate the relevant tracking documents pinning down specific actions leading up to and including the date and timing of the robbery.

The diamonds had left South Africa for Amsterdam, carried by a courier, a twenty-year veteran with Gemtec. He was the principal trusted mule, escorted by one other personnel on every shipment flight, but not always the same companion. Standard operational procedure dictated the courier only received advice at the last moment for plane schedules.

The security company pre-advised Customs thirty minutes before the expected plane arrival, making passage a simple matter. A general monetary bond arrangement posted with the Customs Department minimized the time and formalities for bringing the gems into Holland. The process completed with the courier and his companion delivering the goods into the security company's control simply by climbing into the armoured vehicle. The final destination of the diamonds remained confidential, passed only from Bergman to the head of operations at the security firm.

On the day of the robbery, weather caused a slight delay to the flight from South Africa. The courier and his escort de-planed and processed through the special

Customs area as per normal. On completion of formalities, the pair boarded the Guardwell security van and headed off towards Utrecht.

The guard who stepped out of the truck with the courier remembered the attackers' commands being in Dutch and was also certain two of the robbers shouting to the others to get on the motorbikes spoke in Chinese.

At several points in the narrative, Jack asked Nils to repeat descriptions and details. He wanted to miss nothing. Not surprisingly, Bergman had the facts down to the finest nuance, after constant repetitions to the detectives from Utrecht and Amsterdam.

The briefing continued without a break until halfway through the evening, at which point they decided to finish for the day. Jack now had a strong grip of the sequence covering the trail from the time the diamonds departed South Africa until they passed into the hands of the assailants.

The reiteration of facts and cross-reference, piece by piece in the chain, left him mentally tired. He was glad to get back to his hotel and put his head down.

CHAPTER 8

The first week in Gemtec's offices kept Jack fully engaged.

Nils Bergman continued to be scrupulous in the supply of detail required, whatever the Scotsman demanded. The information covered areas of contact - internal and external. Who knew about the shipment? When did they know? How did they know? Who else did they talk to?

Jack cross-verified where possible. He needed a stack of background tracing on this shit, he reflected. He'd have to double-check on every element, every piece of the process.

At the source was the supplier in South Africa. Jack called the wholesaling company who shipped the gems. Marcus Joran, second top man for Commodity Exports in Johannesburg, responsible for coordination with Gemtec, and their contact point over many years, welcomed the call.

The routine was simple but effective, he explained. Only Joran had details of shipping schedules and the contents up until the day of shipment, a standard theme recurrent across the industry. He normally received a call from Nils Bergman a week or two in advance of shipment date with a specific request for stones. This gave him time to source and aggregate Gemtec's requirements. Nearer to the flight, Nils called again to fix a next-day departure. Then, on the morning of the proposed date, a third call confirmed the named courier detailed to collect and at what time.

"How often do you guys ship to Gemtec?" asked Jack.

"Usually two to three times a year, tops. The value can be quite significant. We don't try to predict when they'll call. They've a practice of staggering demand in different cycles. Some years they'll go several months without ordering, then re-order as soon as a few weeks afterward, impossible to tell."

"Anybody else…anybody, who's familiar with this other than yourself?"

"Not the way we're set up. It's simple and until now it's been flawless. We use the same practice with most of our customers. It keeps things tight and controllable. We're all devastated by the hits on the Gemtec guys. We've dealt with them for many years."

"Okay, thanks Marcus. I'll get back to you for anything else."

* * * * *

The next part of the chain was the security company picking up the precious stones with the courier and his escorts.

The offices of Guardwell Inc located on the outskirts of Schipol Airport cargo complex. A half dozen armoured vans parked along the front wall of the converted warehouse pointed Jack toward the operations hub where the Operations chief, Morg Landis waited for him.

Jack acknowledged a well-organized, clean, efficient, and controlled centre.

"Morg, thanks for seeing me. I understand this might be a bit awkward for you guys. I assure you I'll ask nothing that'll compromise your business."

The older man seemed relaxed at Jack's presence. "No problem. We all want to pin the bastards who did this stuff. I also knew Roddie Bell at Securimax. I bet you ten to a penny the same mob pulled that one too. We'll cooperate to the hilt."

Jack smiled his appreciation. "Thanks. Yeah, I think we all knew Roddie, one of the best. So, can you walk me through how the communication sequence worked on the day of the hit?"

Landis leaned forward across his desk towards his counterpart.

"Our arrangement with Gemtec means we're on twelve-hour notice to pick up at Schipol for immediate onward delivery anywhere in Holland. I'm personally responsible for receiving the calls and mobilizing the armoured cars."

"So you're the one who gets the heads-up on the destination for the deliveries?" asked Jack.

"Yes I am," replied the security man. "Nils Bergman rings me when the flight's about to arrive. He tells me where to deliver, the first notice anyone at Guardwell gets for the final home for the goods. I then call the van to tell the team leader the address after picking up the courier with his package. That's how tight Gemtec wants it and we respect that. The rest you know already. That's all we got. No room for loose tongues in there."

"And the only one who calls you from Gemtec is Bergman?"

"Right. Only Bergman. He's good. The guy runs a close ship. It's tight. Very tight."

"Anything else you can think of? Any gut feel?"

"Just a possibility, nothing more," mused Landis. "My security guard is adamant the attackers were Chinese. He picked up at least one, maybe two of them bawling orders to get on the bikes. He knows enough of a difference to tell it was Cantonese. Gemtec and the other big wholesale guys in Holland also run offices across the Far East, including Hong Kong, which is mostly Cantonese. I can't help sense a tie-in. Nothing concrete, I'm afraid."

Jack decided he'd exhausted what he needed from Landis. "Okay, thanks, Morg. You've been very helpful. Can I get back to you if I think of anything else?"

"Sure thing."

"And by the way, I see no reason why Guardwell and ISP can't work together whenever it suits both of us."

Jack held out his hand which Landis shook warmly.

"We'd appreciate that."

* * * * *

Back in his room later at the Hilton, Jack started to tape-record his notes as usual. So far he had confirmation the circle of parties privy to the movement of the diamonds was small. All on a simple need-to-know basis.

Next morning's schedule included a drive to Utrecht to see Nesta Boertinn, the Managing Director of Grussveld, where the attack occurred. Thirty years in the company, elevated all the way through the ranks to the top of the finest diamond-cutting firm in Holland. Jack raised his eyebrows. *What was with these Dutch companies and the longevity of service?*

The telephone disturbed his thoughts and he picked up on the second ring. Jules Townsend gave a brief hello, and came straight to the point.

"Anything worthwhile yet?"

Jack brought him up to date.

"So far, nothing out of the ordinary. I've checked the process trail for the shipment. In the exporter and the security company only single points of contact to trigger movements. Single point of contact also at Gemtec, Nils Bergman. Bergman's totally trusted by Hubert Meiss. He brought Nils in a few years ago. The circle's tight, Jules."

"So what's next?"

"Tomorrow I'm in Utrecht to interview the boss at Grussveld. They're the diamond-cutters for Gemtec and seemingly half of the gems trade in Holland. Bit of a wonder why they haven't been targeted before this. They've been serving Ostman's business for as long as anyone can remember."

Jules fired more questions. "What about the courier and his escort?"

"The escort isn't always the same man every trip, but the courier is usually the same guy. Background checks on the first lad check out clear so far. He was also killed anyway," Jack told him.

"And the courier?"

"Equally clean, a guy named Kaarl Schepl. Fifty plus. Been with Gemtec forever and a day. Kaarl called his escort on the morning of the flight ten minutes after Nils rang him to go collect the gems. That was the first notification on the shipment. The escort who died was a younger man, an office clerk from Gemtec in Johannesburg."

Jules grunted. "Good work, Jack. Sounds pretty thorough."

"Oh, one other thing," Jack remembered. "Gemtec also runs a large network in the Far East, including in Hong Kong. The security guard's sure he recognized the dialect as Cantonese. The courier company boss shared a gut feeling the Cantonese-speaking guys lead back into Hong Kong."

He could sense Jules' interest at the end of the line, even before his chief replied.

"Well, it may fit in with another bit of intelligence that surfaced this morning."

"What?"

"You haven't met May-Ling Wong yet. She heads up our office in Hong Kong and has good street connections. Some of the heist diamonds may have trickled into Hong Kong already." Jules paused. "And you're right. Gemtec, and plenty of the other big diamond players trade there too. I'll ask May-Ling to fly to Amsterdam to join you for a week or so. Maybe she'll surface something further on the Cantonese angle. She's good, Jack. Been with us for ten months now. She can be trusted with all the stuff you find. Brainstorm with her. I'll send her to Holland by tomorrow night. Reserve a room for her. Keep me posted."

"Will do boss. It'll be good to have her here as I sure as hell can't understand a word of Chinese." Jack grinned. "Man, I'm still struggling with English."

* * * * *

The muted strains of the violin came seeping through the mist. From the darkness, the old man stepped forward, arms stretching towards Jack. Blood dripped from each arm, making soundless splashes across a colourless floor. The mouth moved, but no sound came out. The eyes sunk as deep shadows into a hairless skull. Other apparitions formed by the old man's side. Some dressed in battle uniform, some in street clothes from lands far away from Britain. Guerrillas. Some had adult bodies topped with children's faces. Child warriors. The old man was his father, the others only distorted figures, remembered and half-remembered over years of operations in the service of the SAS.

Together they banded and drifted around Jack. Silent. The faces rigid. Piercing eyes that weren't eyes in both the old man and in the others stared toward him. *At* him. *Through* him. *Inside* him. The figures crowded and multiple sets of arms reached out, touching him. Terrified, he wanted to speak. To scream. To say something. To tell them it wasn't his fault. But the Violin Man and the others couldn't hear him…

Jack sat bolt upright, the bedsheets wringing in sweat, his breathing hard. Small gasps. The few seconds for reality to descend filled with the dread which visited him on a constant basis ever since his first professional killing on the streets of Northern Ireland all those years ago. His heart pounded.

Damn. Only a dream. The same bloody nightmare. What's wrong with me, for God's sake?

He let his head sink back on to the pillow and waited for his pulse to return to normal. Fitful, dreamless sleep brought a welcome dawn.

CHAPTER 9

After breakfast Jack took a little over an hour to find his way by hotel car to Grussveld's offices in Utrecht. The firm was located in the middle of Koningslaan, a broad avenue stretching down the eastern perimeter of Wilhelminapark.

A pleasant environment for employees, uncluttered, with only a few neighbouring buildings, it made an ideal spot for a heist. The entry to Grussveld from the roadside parking area was twenty metres away across the concrete walkway. *Easy pickings. Poor bastards didn't stand a snowball's chance in hell, thought Jack.*

The gang had an open target. Jack registered the line of parked cars and lorries along the same side of the avenue as the drop-off point. Easy to keep the getaway motorbikes ready, their presence unnoticed behind different stationary vehicles until the ambush.

The assistant ushered Jack into Nesta Boertinn's suite. Jack noted the low-key ambience. No fancy paintings. Ordinary carpet rugs. Plain furnishing. The Managing Director herself was all business, her handshake firm. A stocky woman in her late fifties, Jack guessed. A simple, brown dress reached down to ankle-length, covering a pair of shoes Jack's mother would have called 'sensible.'

"Thanks for seeing me, Ms Boertinn." Jack looked into the shrewd, grey eyes. "The police and insurance investigators asked you most of the things I'd also like to cover," he began. "But it's important for me to determine if I can eliminate anything from the enquiries as we try to get to the bottom of this."

"This dreadful affair shocked us all," she replied, her voice low and measured. "To my memory, we've never had anything like this at Grussveld. I'll be glad to try to answer you."

Jack went through the usual questions. "I'm trying to tie down the timings of the notification of the shipment to Grussveld. Who was in the loop, and at what specific times?"

Nesta Boertinn nodded. "I understand. I received the notice from Mr Bergman on the morning of the delivery. He advised me to expect it sometime before noon the same day. That's standard operating practice with Gemtec. It's worked that way for years without any hitch."

"And then you alerted…?"

"I told our head of goods reception who's in charge of the safety vault. Normally he would receive the courier at our secure receiving area just inside the building downstairs, at the left hand side."

"Did he have any prior knowledge of the shipment's arrival?" Jack enquired, expecting the answer he got.

"Absolutely not." Nesta was adamant. "Even I don't learn about it until Mr Bergman advises me. In the unlikely event I wouldn't be available to take his call, the head of goods reception as back-up officer is fully authorized to act on the instructions in my place. However, that's never been necessary. I've always handled the liaison with Mr Bergman direct."

Jack nodded. "When were you made aware the delivery had been hijacked?"

"Oh, I think only a minute or so after the attackers disappeared. My assistant came screaming into my office. Two men had been shot, Mr Calder, causing a great deal of alarm, and panic, of course."

"And you called Nils Bergman to advise him what had happened?"

"Yes. He was horrified, naturally. We all were."

Jack continued with his standard enquiries. "Is there anything else you recall? Any unusual procedural feature? Anyone acting a little out of character or missing work for any pretext?"

"No. The detectives asked the same sort of questions. Nothing out of the ordinary I can think of, and believe me, I've gone over it dozens of times. But, no, nothing." Nesta Boertinn shook her head.

Jack stood up. "Ms Boertinn, you've been patient with me and extremely helpful. I won't take any more of your day. Thank you for your cooperation. I presume it's okay to call you again?"

Next on his list Jack had scheduled time with Deryk Ostman and Hubert Meiss. He arrived ten minutes prior to the two o'clock meeting to find both of them already in Ostman's office.

Jack intended to keep this one brief. He was in no position to provide anything definite to these men at this stage. He needed to clear up something in particular with them.

"Mr Ostman, Hubert, please walk me through the top level process involved when Gemtec decides to buy and import stones?"

Ostman spoke first. "I make the final determination on incoming gem supplies. The traders and manufacturing divisions work to business plans and rolling budgets year round, with fluctuations depending on seasonality and demand off-take. After receipt of my sign-off authority, the head of purchasing division is at liberty to place the general order with our various wholesalers, generally in Johannesburg, but not always exclusively so. His limit for an aggregate purchase is up to five million dollars of merchandise in one shipment. He then liaises with Hubert to organize the logistics process." Ostman looked toward his Head of Security.

"We alert Nils to get the movement details in line," Meiss continued. "He's the only one aware specifically of what moves and when, although, of course, Mr Ostman, myself and the head of purchasing have overall knowledge of what's going on. We've operated in this manner for many years and find it's the best way of securing the integrity of the process."

Jack replied. "I understand, thanks. I wanted to clarify the sequence with you both at this stage."

"Fine," said Ostman. "Hubert, will you excuse us now? I'd like a few words with Mr Calder alone."

Meiss rose at once. "Of course, Mr Ostman. Catch you later Jack."

With his head of security gone, the Dutchman addressed Jack. "As I said before Mr Calder, I want the reports direct to myself. Given Hubert's position in the company and my desire to have your independent assessment on all this, I think it best to keep him at arm's length. That's why I asked him to step out."

Jack met the other man's eyes. "Quite wise. I'm sure he understands and appreciates your position."

Ostman held his gaze. "What've you got for me so far?"

"At this stage, I think we've been able to clear away a lot of static surrounding the hit itself. We're following up on a couple of pointers, including the Chinese angle. In fact, ISP's head of Hong Kong operations is flying in to join me this evening for a week or so to try to develop that line further. According to murmurs, some of the stones have surfaced in Hong Kong, but I can't verify for you at present. I'd rather you kept that information under wraps, sir."

"These exchanges are between you and I only," replied Ostman. "No one else. My father engaged in undercover resistance activity in Amsterdam during the last war. One of the best pieces of advice he ever gave me was the fewer people who know about confidential material the better."

Jack smiled. "Agreed. I'm glad we're on the same wavelength. I'll be heading back now to meet my Hong Kong colleague."

The Dutchman nodded. "Goodbye Mr Calder."

* * * * *

A fax message from Jules waited at the hotel. He had arranged a private breakfast meeting for Jack and May-Ling with Jens Kluvin the following morning at seven-thirty.

Jens and Jules were old acquaintances from Townsend's early days in the SAS. Back then, Jens Kluvin was a senior team leader in the Dutch police rapid response anti-terrorist squad. Together, as pivotal players, they flushed out a red terrorist cell in Rotterdam in an action so well executed it never even made the newspapers.

Kluvin led the raid, with Jules on his heels as they stormed a fortified hideout in a condemned building on the outskirts of the city. The cell of seven men and two women never saw what hit them. Some of the gang raised their weapons as the force entered the area, giving cause enough to open fire on them. None survived.

Kluvin progressed from the rapid response squad to higher levels, becoming head of all serious crime prevention throughout Holland. Headquartered in Amsterdam, his authority reached across the entire country.

Jack looked forward to meeting him.

CHAPTER 10

The voice on the telephone didn't sound as Jack had expected. He'd never had occasion to talk to her before, but now, at a shade after five o'clock, May-Ling had called his room to say she'd checked in and perhaps they could meet downstairs in the coffee lounge. She spoke with the accent of a well-educated, English businesswoman.

"I'll be down in a couple of minutes," he replied, interested to take a look at the Chinese lady running Jules' Far East shop. He entered the room and saw her sitting by herself in a corner table. She rose as he walked toward her.

"Jack? Hello. Good to meet you at last."

"You too," he responded, with a large grin on his face. This wasn't what he'd expected at all.

May-Ling Wong, at five-feet eight, wore immaculate, business attire which did little to camouflage an attractive woman. The high cheek-bones and slightly almond eyes gave away her continent. Shoulder-length, jet-black hair tapered back from her face. The combination of a European body frame and the grace of the Asian manner in her smile was disarming.

Jack gathered himself. "Let's order something, …tea, coffee?"

"Tea for me, thanks." She sat down.

Jack ordered from the waitress and joined May-Ling on the lounge sofa. He grinned again. "Forgive me, I guess I didn't know what to expect when I heard you were coming. I imagined a stern-looking dame with fire-breathing nostrils. Jules picks pretty tough people to run his operations."

She laughed. "You wouldn't be the first to think I'm some sort of soft, little schoolgirl, Jack. Don't judge a book by its cover, huh? A woman boss in this business often takes people by surprise. Hasn't Jules given you my background information already? He filled me in on your history."

Jack shook his head. "I suppose he's been too tied up. I'm delighted you're here. Why don't you fill in the gaps? Excuse the cliché, but what's a nice lady like you doing in a job like this?"

May-Ling offered a smile. "Okay. Here's the potted version. Dad is Hong Kong Chinese. He's a professor at London University. He teaches the Humanities. My mother's also a professor, Welsh, from Swansea. They met at Bristol University when Chinese students in this country were a rare breed. Dad got there on a sponsored scholarship. He did the usual Chinese scholar thing, normal degree followed by a PH.D. Mum retired early about five years back. She does research work on comparative languages. She says that's more fun than trying to drum it into students who're only partly interested in the curriculum. They live in Richmond. Dad hates the weather in England, but relishes the television. Mostly English football. How crazy is that?"

Jack smiled back. "Not so crazy. It could've been Scottish football. Now *that's* crazy. How about a husband?"

"My husband was killed four years ago. I've reverted to my maiden name."

Jack inwardly kicked himself. *God!* He'd opened his mouth and stepped right inside.

"Forgive my stupidity in asking. I'm sorry to hear that."

She shrugged disarmingly. "I think it's good for you to know anyway. Ben worked in the police force in Hong Kong. We both did at the time. He came in from London to join the Anti-Triad Squad. I was on the regular detective beat. About fifteen months after we married, Ben and his guys had an early morning operation involving rival triad gangs. The word on the street warned of a face-off and a possible shoot-out. The police were supposed to get in and grab a bunch of them before it started. Unfortunately, as Ben made his move, the firing began and he caught a bullet, the first man down. Two other policemen were hit, but they survived."

"Did you leave the force?"

"No. I asked for a transfer into Ben's unit. Maybe strange to some people, but it gave me a way to come to terms with Ben's death. I'm half-Chinese and fluent in Cantonese. A woman cop under cover in Hong Kong is a rarity. I was useful to the squad. I stayed for another three years before deciding to join you guys at ISP. Donnie Mullen, a good friend in the Hong Kong force, recommended Jules Townsend to me. Jules is persuasive, so here I am." She spread her hands palms upwards in an open gesture as she finished.

Jack nodded with respect. "Here you are, indeed. You'll be a godsend on the Chinese connection. There's smoke signals rising on that side, and Jules said you'd got a whisper some of the merchandise has found its way into Hong Kong already?"

May-Ling poured more tea before continuing. "A rumour or two. I still have a few favours owed. You know, from time to time we'd turn a blind eye on minor stuff and the street guys would think it a big thing. We'd call in the favour when appropriate. Other times, frankly, we paid for information. Some of the best tip-offs are dropped by one triad gang against another." She took a sip from her cup.

"A lot of turf rivalry exists in Hong Kong. Certain areas, even down to certain streets, belong to specific triad gangs. Some of them are so well-organized, they would put the Mafia to shame. Overseas, in the United States, Europe and Australia, powerful linkages among the localized triads tie in with the gangs back in Hong Kong. Holland has about a dozen identifiable triad organizations, most of them involved in international crime. They run drugs, prostitution and gambling. The whole nine yards."

"Does the style of the heist here ring any bells?" queried Jack.

May-Ling nodded. "Yes. Two outfits doing all of the stuff I've mentioned also specialize in armed robbery. The proceeds from these provides impact cash for some of their other activities. They're the Mok Kwong Cho and the Ching Tan Ka. This is more likely to be the Ching Tan Ka. They're usually much better organized, and certainly better managed."

"Managed?"

"Yes. Don't forget, this is business to these people. Both gangs are sworn enemies. They compete like hell in Hong Kong, and anywhere else they overlap. Sometimes we get open warfare season. A lot of members are killed and businesses hit. It quietens down again for a while, until the next event. The top men in Ching Tan Ka are the Chan brothers. They're nicknamed the Half Moon Twins. Jonnie and Jimmie Half Moon."

"Why?"

"Easy. When they were born, each had an unmissable red crescent birthmark. Jonnie has his on the right of his forehead, Jimmie's is on the left cheek."

"Are these Half Moon brothers in Hong Kong now?"

"Yes."

"Young guys? Old guys?"

"Probably late forties."

"Why don't you arrest them?"

"It's not that simple. Remember, I told you they're highly organized businessmen. They ensure enough layers between themselves and the actual criminal activities. They also have a raft of legal advisers who keep them out of the hands of the police and well away from the law courts."

"Smart crooks, huh?"

"You bet." May-Ling wrinkled her nose. "They launder crime proceeds through hundreds of small, cash businesses in Hong Kong, making it almost impossible to hit them with anything that'll stick. If we got them on a parking fine, even that would be a big deal."

Jack grunted. "Lots of food for thought. Speaking of which, it's almost dinnertime. You feel like eating? They've a fine-dining restaurant here." He signalled for the check.

May-Ling nodded. "Why not? I didn't eat at all on the flight over. I chose sleep as a better attraction than the airline grub."

"Good call. I don't blame you. Let's go."

The steak restaurant provided a welcome change from the room-service menu Jack had been steadily slogging his way through since arriving at the hotel. There's only so many club sandwiches a man can eat in a week.

Over dinner he brought May-Ling up to date with all the details of his meetings thus far. His call to Commodity Exchange in South Africa, the meeting with Morg Landis at the security agency, and with Nesta Boertinn of Grussveld. Lastly, the brief discussion with Deryk Ostman and Hubert Meiss.

He tracked the process one more time from start to finish as he pictured it. May-Ling listened intently as she ate. Relying entirely on memory, Jack laid out his mental notes in between the courses. He traced the conversations with Nils Bergman over the previous week covering the trail of communication links. She interrupted only twice to have him repeat a couple of details.

They treated dinner as strictly business and neither had wine. However, when they'd exhausted the last of the conversation on the heist events, they adjourned to the lounge and both ordered a brandy. Jack was beginning to feel better about the whole Amsterdam business than at any time since his arrival. He sensed May-Ling's presence had brought another excellent professional into the picture. She asked the right questions. Her investigative police training showed. He guessed she'd be a major plus as they moved ahead with the investigations.

He learned indirectly she was in her early thirties and had excelled in her studies in Hong Kong and later at University in England. Over the course of the rest of the evening Jack relaxed even further.

It was close to midnight when they said goodnight. May-Ling really did look weary now. But still attractive…

"See you at breakfast," he said, as she stepped out of the elevator on the floor below his. "Seven-thirty. Private dining salon, just off the main restaurant corridor. Sleep well."

"Goodnight, Jack," came the tired response as May-Ling headed toward her room.

CHAPTER 11

The dawn light streamed in through his room window just before six o'clock, bringing Jack awake.

He always slept with the curtains undrawn so the daybreak acted as his alarm. His routine shower with water as hot as he could bear took only ten minutes. Apart from the recurrent nightmares, he seldom recalled dreams from the night before, but he had the sense he'd had a restless sleep, broken with different images of his father, talking to him in Chinese. Of an English guy called Ben firing guns non-stop with no sound coming from them. Of a large sand-pile of diamonds as big as his fist, tantalizingly out of grasp.

He dismissed the tricks of a tired mind and readied himself to meet Jens Kluvin.

* * * * *

Although they were only three for breakfast, the private salon was laid out with enough food for a dozen. Jack was five minutes early - another of his habits - but found both Kluvin and May-Ling had preceded him. The Dutchman rose and offered a strong handshake.

"Good morning, Jack. A real pleasure to meet you at last. May-Ling and I ordered coffee already."

Jack returned the greeting. "The same here. I understand you and Jules go back quite a way. Morning, May-Ling, I trust you had a good night's sleep?"

"Thanks. Yes. Slept like a baby." She looked even more attractive than the previous evening. Jens was already comfortable in her company.

The taller man spoke, "It seems May-Ling and I have a common acquaintance, Jack. Donnie Mullen, or more correctly, Detective Chief Inspector Donnie Mullen. He and I meet often in anti-crime conferences around the globe. In fact, we talk about once a month on the Chinese crime syndicates."

May-Ling turned to Jack. "Donnie was the guy I told you about last night who introduced me to Jules. He was my boss for the three years in the Anti-Triad Squad, and a good friend after Ben died. He still is."

"I've found the longer I'm in this business, the more it resembles a large village," continued Jens. "The networking is incredibly simple. It's not who you know, it's who knows you," he added with a smile. "I know Mick Jagger, but he doesn't know me, so that's no good. Get what I mean?"

"Yes," laughed Jack. "Shall we eat?"

They tackled the buffet table while Jack observed Kluvin. The man was in his mid-fifties, fit as a fiddle, probably gym regimen, like a lot of the former rapid-reaction guys. Once there, seldom forgotten. Grey sides to the hair, but healthy features. The Dutch campaign against heavy crime had a good torch-bearer.

"Jules asked for this meeting to brainstorm together," said the policeman. "None of us holds the monopoly on solutions. Anything I can do to assist you will be done. I've already told my people in Utrecht, Rotterdam and here in Amsterdam if you call them you can have access to everything we have. Here's the contact names and numbers for the heads in these stations." He handed Jack a sheet of paper with the details handwritten.

"Appreciated," said Jack. "On our side I can share my current findings. Apart from Jules of course, I report only to Deryk Ostman, the owner of Gemtec. However, I'm certain he'd not object to you being in the loop. He seemed cut up about the deaths of his employees."

"Yes." Kluvin nodded. "I'd figure that. My father and he were together in the resistance movement during the war. The family is straight. Dead straight. Deryk Ostman wouldn't be a problem."

Jack leant forward. "Let me track across what I've done already."

He spent almost forty minutes repeating the same details to Jens he'd shared with May-Ling over dinner. She listened for the second time, impressed with Jack's orderly mind and how clearly he set out his findings to the police chief. He missed nothing and added nothing from the previous night.

Kluvin waited without interruption until Jack finished. He asked, "Where does it lead you, Jack?"

"Well, everything points to an inside collaboration of some sort," Jack responded. "It'll be helpful if I can somehow get access to the outgoing telephone records of the top four guys at Gemtec covering the day before and the day of the robbery."

"Top four?"

"Ostman, Meiss, Bergman and a guy called Weiner, the head of purchasing."

Jens smiled. "You'd make a good cop, Jack."

He opened his attaché case and handed over a transparent folder. "Ostman, Meiss, Bergman, Weiner. Telephone calls out of Gemtec, going back for two weeks prior to the hit, as well as the day of the heist, and the day after. First things my guys looked for. You can keep the copies."

Jack nodded in appreciation. "How did you know I'd ask for these?"

"I guessed you'd be thorough. Being thorough means you'd need the communication connects?"

Jack laughed. May-Ling also smiled.

"Let me do the executive summary of the telephone calls for you. If you'll get us some more coffee?" added the Dutchman.

"Sure. Anything for the chief of police, now doubling as my detective studies trainer. You got it," Jack replied, still laughing.

Jens nodded towards the paper in Jack's hand. "Ostman. Every call checks out as legitimate business including a couple to his daughter in Ontario. She runs their North American operations. Meiss, surprisingly, no external calls made at all. He says he's not in the habit of initiating calls outside of Gemtec."

"That leaves Bergman and Weiner. I've not interviewed Weiner yet," said Jack.

"Forget Weiner. He made no calls. Bergman handles all of the outside logistics as…"

"…as that's how they've done it for years," Jack finished the sentence for him.

"…as that's how they've done it for years," repeated Kluvin with a wry smile.

Jack was thoughtful. "Which leaves Nils Bergman, the only common point of external contact with South Africa, with the local security carrier here in Holland, and with Grussveld, the ultimate destination for the diamonds. But being the only point of contact doesn't necessarily make him guilty. He told me he made seven external calls during the two days. Three to Joran at Commodity Exports. The first to confirm the amount of stones to ship. The second to agree the flight schedule and the third, the standard contact to authorize handing the package to Kaarl Schepl, the courier. One call to Schepl to get organized to travel, makes four. One to Morg Landis at Guardwell to get the van on standby at Schipol, five. One to Nesta Boertinn at Grussveld to expect the shipment gets us to six."

"That leaves the final call," Jack continued. "Made on the morning of the hit to a company called Pan Asia Export Company Limited – an outfit exporting to, get this, Asia, mainly to Hong Kong. Nils claims he was soliciting quotations for shipping out a sizable amount of merchandise to Hong Kong in the next week or so." He paused as May-Ling poured more coffee for them. "The annual Jewellery and Gems Exhibition starts in a couple weeks, one of the biggest events in the industry. Gemtec, and the other big players from across the globe always showcase. The show attracts a hundred thousand visitors including corporate buyers and large private collectors."

"So Bergman's guilty of nothing more than being a telephone caller," said Kluvin.

"Right," replied Jack. "And he's a former professional soldier. He's also an excellent administrator. If he was an inside collaborator he'd realize the first thing checked would be the telephone lists. Hardly likely to put himself at that kind of risk, which leaves us still looking."

Jens Kluvin clucked at his host and hostess.

"Good, Jack. Very good. We made the same telephone checks, and ran the ruler over Nils Bergman. The call to Pan Asia also checks out. The guy on the other side is

Chinese, been in Amsterdam for many years, a Mr Choi. He's the head of Marketing for Pan Asia, we visited him. Everything rings clean, the company seems above board. They've been in business here since 1971."

Jack nodded. "Any trace on the motorbikes?"

"Nothing yet. There's more motorbikes than cars in this country. The bikes split up after leaving the scene. A group of them together with a posse of guys all dressed in black would've stood out like a sore thumb. Individual bikes wouldn't get a second look. This was a well-planned hit, Jack. We've got a lot of listeners on the street but nothing audible yet. We'll keep listening. We're also beating the streets on the Rotterdam case. The one that took out Roddie Bell."

Jack raised an eyebrow. "You knew Roddie, too?"

"Yes," Jens sighed. "Roddie, Jules and I often used to trade drinks back in the old days. So far we've found no tie-in for the two events. No apparent links other than security companies being in the middle of both. Maybe just coincidence."

"A whisper in Hong Kong says this might be linked to the Ching Tan Ka triads,'" put in May-Ling. "Are they big in Holland, Jens?"

He turned toward her, "Yes, we're aware the Ching Tan Ka are here, but so are several other groups connected with Hong Kong and Taiwan. Just how large they are we've not yet been able to guage. So far, we've had nothing of any significance on these guys. Nothing we could pursue. I understand they maintain a low profile."

"Yes," agreed May-Ling. "Until now, we've never pinned anything on them either. But we keep looking."

"Armed heists are a bit of a novelty in Holland," said Jens. "These two jobs were the work of serious long-term planning. The execution was well-organized, the killings almost matter of fact. They were prepared to kill. That's not too common here either."

"Murder's standard practice with the triad gangs," replied May-Ling. "I'll try to dig locally to help with that angle."

The Dutchman nodded his thanks. "Good. Again, if you need any feedback from my guys, Jack's got the numbers to call."

"Jens. A real pleasure," said Jack, rising to his feet.

"Same here. I must get going my friends. I've a meeting at eleven. Great to meet you both. Let's keep in touch." Kluvin exchanged warm handshakes and left.

The ease with which Kluvin had just given him the green light to investigate on the Rotterdam heist as well as the Utrecht hit impressed Jack.

So far there was apparently no link between the two events, but his gut screamed something else.

CHAPTER 12

In the afternoon they drove to Rotterdam. The journey passed quickly and within an hour and a half they parked the hired Renault in the driveway of Police Headquarters. After parting company with Jens Kluvin, a call to Senior Detective Bram Carbet had secured a three o'clock meeting.

Younger than Kluvin by about twelve years, Carbet welcomed Jack and May-Ling as warmly as Jens had anticipated. Bram Carbet's career in the Rotterdam detective force traced back almost a decade, the last three as Chief of Station. The smell of coffee greeted them as they entered a small conference room. Documents and files filled the centre of the table. The detective had obviously been briefed by his superior commander to be as helpful as possible.

There's no way the Securimax hit in Rotterdam isn't connected with the Gemtec heist, Jack thought. But where's the bloody linkage? Get that, and we'd be halfway solved. Jens Kluvin's comment about armed robbery not being common in Holland stuck in his mind. There had to be a connection. Two incidents within a week of each other seemed less and less a coincidence.

After the heist and killing, Carbet had led the local investigation. According to Jens, all the information was at his fingertips.

"We appreciate you seeing us at short notice, Bram," said Jack. "Jens told us you're the best in the business and you'd be able to brief us on what went down at the warehouse."

"Don't know about being the best in the business," Carbet smiled disarmingly.   "Jens Kluvin's got a lot of good people around him. He attracts the type. He called me while you were driving here. Says you haven't been filled in yet on the details of our case?"

Jack pulled a face. "We've got the overview but I thought it'd be helpful to compare the elements in the two hits to see if there's any match?"

The Dutchman man nodded. "Seems reasonable. Where do you want to start then?"

Jack began to rapid-fire questions. "Getaway vehicles in Utrecht were motorbikes. Yours?"

"Two vans, as far as we can tell, dark-coloured."

"Disguises, Halloween masks. Yours?"

"Assortment of ski masks, eyes only showing."

"Guns in Utrecht were Uzis. Yours?"

"AK47s. No Uzis."

"Anyone hear Chinese?"

"No again, Jack. Only Dutch."

"How about the clothing? All black?"

"Negative. We have various colours, none very distinctive, but certainly not all black. We've a security camera film I'll run for you in a minute - you can check for yourselves."

"How much did they take?" asked May-Ling.

"Four point two million dollars."

Jack whistled. "Some hit. No word from the street yet? Nobody trying to fence any of it?"

Carbet shook his head. "With something this big, it's going overseas, for sure. Probably melted down, then peddled. The Dutch market is too much of a clique. The whole place would know if any surfaced here."

"Which company shipped in to Securimax?" May-Ling looked at Carbet.

"Alliance Trading Company Limited, based here in Rotterdam. We checked them out too, of course. Long-time working relationship with Securimax. Been around for fifteen years in this business. They have branches world-wide."

"Including Hong Kong?"

Carbet nodded. "Here's their telephone number," he added, anticipating the follow-up question. "The main contact guy is Chinese, a Mr Kai. He's been in Holland for many years. Carries dual citizenship - Dutch and Hong Kong. Most of the international companies with Far Eastern connections have Chinese in charge of operations. Here, let me run the tape for you."

A small television set and player sat at the end of the table. He clicked a monitor. The CCTV film was a little grainy, but clear enough to capture the action. Jack and May-Ling watched intently and asked to run it a couple of times more.

The robbery took just short of three and a half minutes as Carbet had indicated. So far the speed of execution was the only obvious similarity with the Utrecht case, fast, and well organized. Both gangs knew exactly what every member had to do. Jack had seen live shootings close-up several times, but he flinched each time his former buddy, Roddie Bell, went down.

He glanced swiftly at May-Ling, remembering her husband had also been taken out this way. She seemed to be okay.

Tough lady.

They ran the film a few extra times. Carbet clicked the machine to extract the tape and handed it to Jack. "Jens said you'd ask for a copy."

"Thanks. Any leads so far?"

"It points to inside intelligence of some sort. The trouble is, we've ruled out just about every possible link.

All clean. We'll keep on it of course, but it would be good to get a break in this somewhere."

Jack nodded. "Thanks, Bram. I don't think there's much else to trouble you with. That was comprehensive. We'll head back to Amsterdam now, but if you're up our way soon, give me a call. We owe you a drink."

* * * * *

The Guardwell security guard ordered to the ground during the Utrecht attack made himself available to Jack the next morning. He was the sole witness on the day of the robbery.

In the hotel room, Jack set up the television monitor to play the copy tape for his visitor. He wanted to find out if the guard could pick up on any similarities the rest of them had missed.

Peter Dewer had been with Guardwell for six years. Shaken up by the shooting experience, he had shown some guts by getting back into service the next day.

Jack's tone was friendly. "From what I understand, Peter, Grussveld has never considered the need for security cameras in their building. Consequently, we've no tapes from the Utrecht hit you were involved in, but I'd like you to watch this clip from the Rotterdam warehouse. If you spot anything that matches up yell out."

"Be glad to. Let's have a look."

Jack observed him closely. A young guy, no older than twenty-eight or so. Alert. Keen. Good material.

They ran the film. Dewer gave a start at the point where Roddie Bell was shot. The tape finished and he sat still, almost hypnotised.

"Anything?" queried Jack.

"No. Sorry. Nothing obvious. The whole thing looks different. The guns aren't the same. Can you show me once more?"

"As many times as you like." Jack switched to 'play'.

It finished the second time, and Dewer pointed. "Hold on. Re-run it again, near the end, let me see that again."

Jack did as asked.

At about the three-minute mark, Dewer shouted. "Freeze it there! No, back a little. There. Yes. There."

"What is it?"

"You see the hand-signal from this guy?" The man on the film indicated the classic *Time Out* sign by making a *T* shape with the fingers of one hand pointing into the palm of the other.

"So?"

"That's the same signal one of the guys in Utrecht made when he started getting them on to the bikes. In fact,

I could swear I recognize the body shape. That's the same guy."

Jack shook his hand. "Thank you, Peter. You're a gutsy guy. If you're ever looking for a job in this business, you come and talk to me."

He showed the young man to the door and said goodbye, staring thoughtfully at the empty screen.

Not a hundred percent sign to hang a case on, but Peter Dewer seemed sure of the likeness. If he was right, it would confirm the same gang pulled off both jobs.

But why no other common traits in the hits?

CHAPTER 13

A few days later, Jules called midway through the afternoon. As always, he wanted to listen first to Jack's report on progress.

Jack was happy to give him the update. "We met your man Jens. Terrific help on the ground here. He got us a face to face with their guy in Rotterdam. I think we may have a link between the two hits. One of the guards involved in the Utrecht take down is almost sure the gang was the same for both places. Plus a couple of armoured robberies in a week with none for the previous seven or eight years seems a bit tight to me."

"You're covering the bases well, So well, in fact, I'm pleased to tell you Ostman agreed yesterday to give ISP the contract for all his global security arrangements."

The pride in his boss's voice didn't escape Jack.

"I don't have to repeat what a major account this is," Jules continued. "We take over fully at the end of this month. Great work. He obviously likes the way you've gone about the review so far."

"Terrific news. You been working this guy over for the last few weeks?"

Jules chuckled. "Part of my job, playing the corporate

SEUMAS GALLACHER

business buddy tying up the big fellows, while you guys do the real work."

Jack smiled, well aware leaving the real work to others wasn't Julian Townsend's style. A front leader in everything he did, the man wouldn't know how to be any different.

"You'll coordinate with Meiss and Ostman to figure out the handover details from Guardwell," Jules said. "We also need a fuller handle on how they interface with their other branches around the world. It's going to take some changes on our side to cope with their reach."

"Right," replied Jack, as he did a mental check-off of Gemtec's operational centres. In Europe they were in Amsterdam, Frankfurt, London, and Paris. North America was covered out of Toronto, the Indian market out of Calcutta and in the Far East, Singapore and Hong Kong. "We'll need some thinking on coverage logistics."

"True," said Jules. "Their main hubs are Amsterdam, London and Hong Kong. The UK and the Far East I think we've got pretty much locked down. We'll need to staff up in Amsterdam rather than try to manage out of London as we do now. As far as personnel go, May-Ling is capable of handling the Hong Kong piece and Singapore," Jules continued. "We may choose to do India and the rest of the sub-continent from London. Toronto certainly from London. Frankfurt and Paris out of Amsterdam. I've got some prospective names to head up Amsterdam, and probably a new face in London to free up Malky a bit. I think you and he are going to be needed a level or two up from here, helping me regionally as the business grows."

Jack caught his enthusiasm. "Sounds good. Let's discuss further when I'm back in London."

"Agreed. How's May-Ling doing?"

"She's calling the Chinese guy at Pan Asia, the shippers. She's checking him out, although I don't think he's aware of that."

"Okay, keep me in the loop. I'll be in touch soon. Ostman says you can start on the handover issues with Hubert any time you like. I suggest you fix for tomorrow."

"On it.'

* * * * *

May-Ling was as pleased as Jack to learn about the Gemtec contract. They were having dinner in the same restaurant as on the first night they'd met.

"I think Jules was keen to land this one," she said. "It'll be ISP's first full global account."

"Yes, he's been talking for a while now as to where we take the business next," Jack told her. "He's figuring out how we get geographic coverage. We'll want a few top-flight hires to run some of the new stuff. I've already started on fresh blood. I made a job offer to Peter Dewer from Guardwell today. He'd be a fine coordinator and security head for us."

May-Ling said, "It's going to require a lot of tying down. There's tons of moving parts but it'll act as a magnet for other accounts to follow suit. I'm getting plenty of interest generated in Hong Kong and the rest of Asia."

"Speaking of Asia, how did you get on with your Mr Choi today?" Jack topped up her water glass.

"Reasonably well, I think. He was quite open on the phone with me. We chatted in Cantonese. I told him I was with a new precious stones and jewellery sourcing business here in Amsterdam, but looking to supply retail customer outlets in Hong Kong. I asked about Pan Asia's ability to service our shipping needs, price ranges, and so on. He sounded professional and polite. I hinted we'd be starting off in a modest way, no more than say fifty thousand US dollar value movements to begin with, expecting bigger growth as the business developed."

"Did he bite?"

"Yes. He said such amounts are commonplace in their trade. Pan Asia has many clients in the range. They also handle shipments up to a million dollars. That fits in with what Bergman had indicated too, about shipment capabilities for the Trade Show."

"Anything else interesting?"

"I asked him who his counterparty agency is in Hong

Kong. He said that's his parent company, Asia Fortune Shippers Company Limited. I thanked him for his help and he asked where to deliver the company's brochure for me to read. I told him I was billeted at the Hilton for this trip, and he could send the stuff to the hotel. He'll have it delivered by this evening. Service, huh?"

Jack smiled at her. "So now what?"

"The 'now what?' is we check out the parent company. Companies registry in Hong Kong," May-Ling grinned. "Remember, my backyard? Let's see what we find."

"Good lady. Tomorrow I think we spend time with Hubert Meiss to get the ball rolling. Nils should also be around. He's the guy who handles all the logistics for Gemtec. I'll be interested to get a sense of your woman's instinct on him."

"Jack, let me tell you the woman's instinct thing is no different from a man's instinct. You either feel something's wrong or you don't. There's no difference for gender." She flashed another of those beautiful smiles.

Something stirred inside Jack.

No difference for gender? She must be kidding.

May-Ling, you are a gorgeous difference…

CHAPTER 14

It was roll-up-the-sleeves time. Jack and May-Ling spent the balance of the week with Meiss and Bergman coordinating the interface requirements prior to the impending transition from Guardwell.

A smooth handover execution by month-end was imperative for ISP. Jack asked Malky to consider how many people he could spare from London to kick-start things in Holland, without blowing away the business back home.

Malky sent over two senior ISP managers on secondment, on the starting day of deliberations. By the end of the week, ISP had its own vehicles on the ground in Holland, also manned with security staff from London. A programme for local hirings had begun.

Jack insisted on taking part in every interview. He knew the kind of people needed to safeguard their customers' interests and those who could be relied upon in situations of danger to ISP's own personnel.

He'd learned from Jules Townsend that hands-on management beat every other approach to most things.

CHAPTER 15

"Anything new?" asked Jack. May-Ling had started to review some of the documentation relating to the two robberies. She now sat opposite him in the coffee lounge at the hotel, late in the evening of what had been a long working Saturday after days of wall to wall hiring interviews.

May-Ling was upbeat. "Yes, a couple of things I think'll interest you. I retraced the telephone call list Jens gave us over breakfast. You remember the records went back a couple of weeks before the Utrecht take out?"

Jack murmured in agreement as she continued, "We only focused on the calls for the day before the hit and the day of the incident itself, right?"

"Right."

May-Ling looked animated. "I went through the lists again and found something interesting. On the morning of the Rotterdam heist, several days before the Gemtec robbery, the telephone account from Nils Bergman's office shows a call to a number in Rotterdam which seemed a little familiar."

Jack pulled a face. "Come on, stop pulling me along, whose?"

"The direct line for Mr Kai at Alliance Trading, the shippers for the bullion."

Jack raised an eyebrow. "Did you check our notes if Bram Carbet questioned Bergman on that one?"

May-Ling nodded. "'Yes I checked. He doesn't mention it anywhere. I reckon Bergman's answer would be he asked them for the same kind of shipping details as he did from Pan Asia to ship goods to the Hong Kong Trade Show. I've mentioned this to no-one yet."

"Interesting. You said you had a couple of things. What else?"

"I called Mr Kai at Alliance Trading on that same number. Of course I made no mention of Bergman or any of the other stuff. I had a similar conversation in Cantonese to the one I had with Mr Choi at Pan Asia. I explained my company's needs for shipping services for gems and precious stones to Hong Kong. Turns out Alliance Trading Company Limited does pretty much similar business to Pan Asia. They also have a Hong Kong parent company. The name is Star Fortune Shippers. Ring any bells?" she teased.

Jack grimaced. "Not really. Should I hear ringing?"

"The Hong Kong parent company of Pan Asia is Asia Fortune Shippers. Both carry the 'Fortune' tag."

"So?"

May-Ling picked up the last of her coffee. "In many instances, companies with links retain common names. Both are here in Holland, both hold Hong Kong parentage and these parent companies have 'Fortune' in the tag line."

Jack leant back and stared at her. "Where does this lead us, then?"

"It's too late now to call Hong Kong, everyone's asleep," replied May-Ling. "I sent a fax to the office asking them to check out if these two parent companies share a common holding company."

"And if they do?"

May-Ling shook her head. "At this stage I'm fishing, but if we find a link, we start digging again. We won't know until tomorrow, so let's sleep on it."

The idea of sleeping on it brought a flicker across his mind. He realised May-Ling aroused something within him that had been absent for too long. In the past his response would have been to offer to sleep on it with her. *But hell, she's a colleague for God's sake, leave it alone, man.* May-Ling caught the look and the hesitation but didn't respond. The moment passed.

"Sure," he said. "Let's catch up over breakfast, say seven-thirty?"

CHAPTER 16

The breakfast room was only half full when they arrived within minutes of each other the following morning. They commandeered a vacant corner table and both ordered continental breakfast. May-Ling waved a couple of sheets of paper at Jack.

"What're they?"

"Delivered this morning. The fax information from Hong Kong on our famous Fortune parent companies."

"Good," mumbled Jack through a mouthful of toast.

"Read this," she commanded, handing the fax sheets across.

"What do they say?" he queried, as he began to read.

May-Ling reverted to her business tone. "It tells us my thinking was bang on the money. Star Fortune Shippers Company Limited and Asia Fortune Shippers Company both have the same holding company ownership. The holding company is Fortune Holdings Company Limited in Hong Kong. Along with about forty other sister companies, all with 'Fortune' in the title."

"So far, so good," said Jack.

"It gets better. Most of the directors of the Hong Kong entities have ties to each other, which isn't uncommon. Usually they're family related."

"Next?" Jack could hardly hide his impatience.

"I'm familiar with the family names on here, Jack. They're all related to the Chans."

Jack frowned. "I thought there were thousands of families called Chan in Hong Kong."

"These Chans are related to Ming Wo Chan and Pang Yee Chan - otherwise known as Jimmie and Jonnie Half Moon - the triad guys I told you about," May-Ling said triumphantly. "Neither of the brothers themselves list as directors, but believe me, they call the shots."

Jack almost dropped his coffee cup. "May-Ling, that's brilliant. You've nailed the connection. Bingo!"

She smiled. "More than the Chinese link. I think it just raised the ante on Nils Bergman's involvement. I'm certain it confirms he's the insider."

"God, I hadn't thought that fast," Jack said, looking at her with undisguised admiration.

"Oh, I hadn't either," she replied, laughing. "I started out suspecting he had more to do with it, but we'd nothing to tie him on to. Bergman's calls to Mr Choi and Mr Kai seem less innocent now with this link. The fishing for the corporate stuff we would've done anyway, to eliminate things. We've got a home run instead. Also, try this for size. Two heists with every single element different. No overlaps on guns, dress, vehicles. What're the odds? It could be the perpetrators trying too hard to make it seem there's no connection. Classic red herring trail. I'm certain the same mob did both hits."

Jack whistled. "Why the hell didn't I think of that? Too obvious, huh? I think we have to share this with Jens Kluvin."

"Right, and then with Deryk Ostman. You give Jens a head-start first, correct?"

"Absolutely," he agreed, reaching for the telephone. Jens Kluvin was at home when the call reached him. "Good morning, Jens," Jack started. "May-Ling's found a connection between the two hits. The shipping companies for each of the deliveries have a common thread back into Hong Kong." He told Jens about Bergman calling both Choi and Kai. "Too much coincidence for a simple mind like mine," he finished. "What do you think?"

"That's enough for me to pull him in," said the police boss. "I had my own suspicions, I must say, regarding our Mr Bergman, but nothing substantive to move on until this. Great work."

"You going to bring him in now?"

"Yes. We have his residential address already. We'll pick him up in less than an hour. I'll keep you posted. Thanks, Jack. Pretty switched on lady, your Miss Wong."

She was certainly looking pretty switched on last night, thought Jack, remembering how close he'd come to overstepping the mark.

"Jens says he'll revert when we can inform Deryk Ostman." Jack told May-Ling. "Probably take him about an hour."

"In which case, I guess we've time to enjoy the rest of our breakfast," she murmured. "More coffee?" She reached across to fill Jack's cup. This Sunday was beginning well, he thought.

CHAPTER 17

Jens Kluvin seldom had a free weekend without a barrage of paper work to consume his Sundays. This one was no different. The call from Jack Calder gave him a welcome excuse to put the files aside. The opportunity to postpone the drudge of documents and join his men in the field was never to be missed if he could help it.

He called Detective Inspector Dick de Jong, his number two, to explain what was needed.

"Send one car to Gemtec in case he's gone to work today - I understand he's a bit of a workaholic," he ordered. "I'll rendezvous with you at his residence in about twenty minutes."

"Yes, boss. On the way."

"Dick, ensure our officers are armed. Bergman was a trained mercenary. We only want to ask him in for questioning at this stage, no mishaps, okay?"

"Understood, boss."

* * * * *

Bergman lived in a block of flats in the Groenelaan district of Amstelveen, a middle-class area five minutes drive from Schiphol Airport. Heavy-duty crime never disturbed the streets of Groenelaan, a typically peaceful, suburban district. No need to use warning sirens or speed through light Sunday traffic to get there.

Jens parked his vehicle at the side of the block and joined Dick and his team of three officers, all in plain clothes, ready and waiting for his instructions.

"Good morning, boys. Morning, Dick."

"Good morning, sir," came the chorus.

"Okay, lads. We want this done nice and easy. Dick, you take one of your men to the rear and get up the service stair. His unit's on the second floor, flat number six. One of you come in with me at the front, and you stay near the vehicles as point man," he said, gesturing to the fourth officer. "No action at the back of the unit unless you hear my command. Understood?"

"Copy sir," said de Jong, as the others nodded acknowledgement.

The front entrance to the building led into an elevator bank just beside the usual personalized mail-boxes on the left hand wall. Jens noted in passing the slot for flat number 206 was empty. A middle-aged caretaker was engrossed in his Sunday newspaper as they approached the elevators. He offered no greeting nor any enquiry as to their presence.

So much for paid security, thought Jens. One might have expected better for a security honcho's living quarters.

Jens and the officer climbed the stairs toward the second floor level. Scattered debris and old newspapers on the landing indicated a tenement lacking high-class cleaning and maintenance.

Jens frowned. Rentals here had to be pretty low. *Didn't the guy earn better than this?*

An array of pot plants stood sentry at the door of unit 206, but they were noticeably the hardy annual type, requiring no daily attention to keep them thriving. Jens pressed the doorbell and moved slightly to one side of the line of sight from its opening edge. The officer with him stayed half a man's length on the other side. No cross-fire angle. There was no reply. He rang the bell a second time and listened for any sound of movement from inside. Nothing. A third ring also brought nothing.

This was not good.

"Stay here until I get back," Jens instructed the officer, and retreated along the landing.

In moments he was on the ground floor, interrupting the caretaker's interest in the sports pages. "Good morning."

"Good morning," came the lazy reply, until the man saw the badge held in the large fist a few inches from his face. He hurriedly discarded the newspaper.

"Sir. What can I do for you?"

"Mr Bergman. Flat 206. Did he leave the building this morning?"

"Mr Bergman, sir? I can't remember seeing him today, sir. Has something happened to him? Is he in trouble of some kind?"

"Not that I'm aware of, my friend. What's your name?"

"Albert, sir. I'm Albert."

"Well Albert. We're just checking Mr Bergman is, in fact, all right. I'm sure you have the standby keys to all the flats here, including number 206?"

"Yes of course, sir, but I don't know if it's proper for you to open Mr Bergman's flat without his authority," said Albert, flustered. He wasn't sure how to cope with this unexpected intrusion on his Sunday morning routine.

"Oh, I've no intention of me opening his flat, Albert," replied the policeman warmly. "We both know you, as caretaker, have authority to open the flat if you feel it's in the best security interests of your tenants, right? Now, as I'm a senior police officer asking for assistance, surely you want to be as helpful as possible to ensure Mr Bergman, who is after all a visitor to our country, is as secure as we can make him. Reasonable?"

He wasn't about to argue with the bulk of authority in front of him.

A few minutes later, Albert fumbled the spare key into the lock of flat 206 and Jens signalled him to move away. The caretaker started back apprehensively as the officer accompanying Kluvin drew his service gun.

"You can go down to the ground floor now, Albert," Jens said quietly. "Thank you for your help."

The older man hurried away.

Jens led the way carefully through the front entrance, he and his officer sweeping the corridors with their firearms in mutual cover. The unit was empty. Jens unlocked the back door to allow Dick de Jong and his partner to come in.

"No one home," affirmed Jens. The inspection of Bergman's quarters took only minutes. Nothing of unwashed dishes in the kitchen. All tidy. No signs of any struggle anywhere. Each of the two bedrooms and living area normal. A swift check of cupboards and storage areas revealed no luggage.

"No suitcases, Jens. Few hanging clothes in the wardrobes. I wonder if Mr Bergman left on a sudden vacation?" mused de Jong.

"Get one of the men to call into the squad car at Gemtec. Tell me if he's turned up today," replied his boss. The second officer with de Jong retreated to carry out the instruction. It didn't take long to confirm Nils Bergman hadn't arrived at his office, although he'd been expected a few hours earlier.

Jens Kluvin issued his orders. "Leave one of your officers here until further notice, Dick. Meantime, get the sniffer boys out and turn this place over. We're looking for indications of his possible whereabouts. Also, any statements, papers, bank accounts. You know the drill. We can't tell if he's left here of his own volition or been removed by force. The caretaker downstairs probably wouldn't have seen him if he'd walked past him in a clown's outfit. Check with the rest of the neighbours. Any sightings of visitors and so on. Any unusual disturbance or raised voices."

"Right, boss. Consider it done," replied his number two.

Kluvin then sought out Albert once more. "Does Mr Bergman own a car park spot here?"

"Yes, sir, at the rear of the building. I checked it out right now. His car's gone. He drives a Volvo, a dark blue Volvo 740. It's a couple of years old, 1992 model."

"If someone used the back stairway to the car park, is it possible he or she could move up or down without you seeing them?" asked Jens.

"Yes sir. Unless I was standing at the back of the building of course, but usually I'm on duty here at the front." replied Albert.

"Any guests recently? Any calls or messages for him?"

"None, sir. Mr Bergman keeps himself to himself, sir. I can't recall anyone except him in the flat for the last few months. No visitors. And no calls or messages. Do you think he's come to some harm, sir?" The man was shaking now.

"Albert, he's probably just gone on vacation for a while. Anyway, if he shows soon, or anyone comes asking for him, give me a call," said Jens, handing him a plain white card containing nothing but his office telephone number. "And, Albert, thanks. You've been most helpful. It won't be forgotten."

"Anytime, sir, anytime," the caretaker mouthed, as the policeman walked back toward the squad car.

CHAPTER 18

Hubert Meiss drove to Gemtec after receiving the call from Kluvin. The two men were seated in Hubert's office. Jens had called Jack, who was expected soon with May-Ling. Deryk Ostman had cancelled an afternoon appointment and was due at any moment.

"You've worked with Nils Bergman longer than anyone, Mr Meiss," said Jens. "I take it this is unusual for him to be neither at home nor at Gemtec when he told his people to expect him? Ever happened before?"

"Never, Chief Inspector," Meiss replied. "Nils is the kind of guy you set your watch by. Apart from his formal vacations, he hasn't missed a day in four years, and that counts most of the weekends as well. He has no family to speak of. I think he left them behind a whole generation ago."

"Any work issues or irregularity you're aware of?"

"He's not the type of guy who'd have these kinds of problems," Meiss answered. "He's efficient in what he controls here. No issues. No complaints. I'd like to think if he had a grievance on something he'd talk to me."

Jens nodded. "Money pressures? Girlfriends?"

"Again, not to my knowledge. We pay pretty well here for the senior guys, and the annual bonus system is generous. We're all rewarded if the business does well. He doesn't spend much. Not into entertaining. A touch frugal in fact. Living costs must be minimal. I don't believe he'd be in financial trouble," added Meiss, rubbing at his neck.

"His car's not in its usual parking bay, so I'm presuming he drove it away, or someone else has forced him," said Kluvin. "Either way, we've an all-points bulletin out to locate him. We've no way of telling when he left the building, therefore he could've been on the road for hours. That would broaden the area of the search, even well beyond the borders."

The arrival of Ostman, just ahead of Jack and May-Ling, interrupted the conversation.

The Dutch boss took over and spoke first. "Chief Inspector Kluvin, thank you for your call. I got here as soon as possible. May I suggest we move into my office? Hubert, can we organize some drinks and coffee? Miss Wong? Mr Calder? Would you care to follow me please?"

The group reassembled in the chief executive's office. They sat surrounding a large, glass coffee-table from which Ostman cleared the Gemtec brochures and business magazines.

He addressed his chief of security, "Hubert, as I understand things, this is out of character for Bergman. Chief Inspector Kluvin already advised me there's a strong possibility this is tied in to the robbery. What do you make of it?"

"I don't understand any of it yet," replied Meiss, with a shrug of the shoulders. "It's out of character. Perhaps Nils will turn up at any moment with a simple explanation. I told the Chief Inspector, Bergman is one of the most reliable officers in this company. I just can't figure it out."

"Chief Inspector." Ostman turned away from Meiss to address the policeman. "I'm as concerned about the safety and well being of Nils Bergman as I am for my other staff. We've had two fatalities in the last few weeks which weigh heavily on this company. I have no desire to see any more. Can you elaborate on your sense this is tied in with the robbery?"

Jack caught a swift narrowing of the eyes from Kluvin as Ostman put the question to him.

"At the moment, Mr Ostman, I can reveal only certain circumstantial elements of our findings. We've reason to think there may be a connection with a shipping company which transports diamonds and precious cargoes, and the appearance of some of the stones in the Far East. Mr Bergman, however innocently, was the intermediary for Gemtec with that company. At present we keep an open mind. His car is missing and he's neither at home nor here at Gemtec, the only two addresses we'd expect to find him at today." Jens stopped.

The policeman had not specifically mentioned Hong Kong, nor the connection by name with Alliance Trading, the shippers for the bullion involved in the other heist.

This was one clever cop, thought Jack.

Kluvin didn't seek to ask nor invite any further questions from these gentlemen, keeping his horizon open.

Jack decided to intercede. "Hubert, what other security shipments in or out do you expect in the next few days? I recommend they be cancelled until we figure out how to manage this in the absence of Nils."

"None. We're not due to ship anything until we start the build-up of shipments to Hong Kong for the Trade Fair."

"Good," said Jack. I think we need to review all of the existing shipment arrangements and plan for alternatives. We'd like to start today, if that's feasible?"

"Agreed," interjected Ostman. "Mr Calder, Miss Wong, your company is taking over in a few days time anyway. Let's use this as the catalyst to handover now. I'll arrange it with the boss of Guardwell. "

He then addressed Meiss. "Hubert, can you get the relevant people to come in this afternoon if they're not already here and make this happen?"

"Of course. Not a problem," Meiss replied.

"Sensible, sir," Jack said to the gems boss. Then to Kluvin, "Chief Inspector, do you have anything else for us?"

Kluvin checked his watch as if intending to leave and replied, "I think we're finished here for the moment. Perhaps we three can move to another room for a little, routine, housekeeping chat? We don't need to be troubling either Mr Ostman or Mr Meiss."

"Okay with you, gentlemen?" asked Jack.

Ostman nodded his agreement. "Chief Inspector, you'll keep me in touch please?"

"Of course, sir. Thank you for your time today."

* * * * *

Kluvin looked thoughtful as they adjourned to the smaller office.

"Nice going, Jens," said Jack. "Information on a need to know basis only, huh?"

"Yes. For the meantime anyway." The policeman opened his arms in a catch-all gesture. "We keep an open mind. Bergman may turn up tomorrow morning with an innocent explanation."

Jack raised his eyebrows. "Somehow I don't think you believe that."

Kluvin didn't answer him. Instead he outlined some of the instructions he'd issued on the way to Gemtec.

"We're checking on the airlines at Schipol, as well as

the airport car parks. Also, discreet background enquiries on the senior personnel at Pan Asia and Alliance Trading. Although with these, as May-Ling has pointed out before, we're dealing with intelligent and careful operators," said Kluvin.

"So you think there *is* a triad connection?" asked May-Ling.

"At this stage I can rule nothing out. Now, as to your observation, I don't believe Nils Bergman is about to re-appear tomorrow, nor indeed at any time soon. And as for Mr Bergman's link to the shippers, my gut tells me he's tied in with this, but we need more to go on than just the excellent intelligence surfaced out of Hong Kong by May-Ling." He shrugged his shoulders, "I can't even guess if he's dead or alive right now. Nothing at his home suggests he's been taken out. Perfectly neat and tidy, almost as if he'd been primed and ready to disappear."

"What else should we be looking for?" asked May-Ling.

"My lads'll run the ruler over Bergman's background as far we can," came the reply. "Like bank accounts with unusual payments. We're finding out where he banks his pay check from Gemtec, but it's unlikely we'll find anything abnormal. More likely to be a private, perhaps coded account somewhere. The other angle is he could've been killed by the people running the gangs. In which case someone else drove his car away."

"Too close a link if some real digging went on?" continued May-Ling. "Either way, it ties him into the robberies?"

"Yes. Either way. The two main theories are either he's done a runner or he's been liquidated."

"Why would he be liquidated?" she asked. Jack listened to the exchange, admiring May-Ling's incisive mind.

"The simple answer could be he's aware enquiries are going on. Your Chinese guys at Pan Asia and Alliance Trading talk to each other and it wouldn't take a genius to figure out where your line of conversation with them was leading, May-Ling. They'd put two and two together and realize you were fishing for a connection. Hence, Nils does a runner after getting the heads-up from them. Or they reckon he's become vulnerable and decide to take him out. Dead men don't talk."

"Oh," she said, with the dawning realisation of the inference. "I hadn't dwelt on that angle."

"Well, it's only a possibility," replied Kluvin.

"What about others in Gemtec being involved?" asked Jack.

"If you mean Ostman or Meiss, nothing leaning toward them at this stage," Kluvin replied, touching Jack on the shoulder. "But as you correctly point out, there's no mileage in sharing everything with them at this juncture.

Weiner, the head of purchasing, checked out clean. Forget about him. A few minor officers operate at one level down from these guys. We're running the scope over them, but again, nothing to indicate collusion with Bergman or anyone else. I don't expect anything from these names."

Jack looked quizzical. "What's the next step? What do you need from us?"

Kluvin gave him his best smile and patted his shoulder again, "I think you guys started the process already by freezing all the existing security arrangements. A fresh approach is always healthy, even when things are trouble-free. Your pending shipments into Hong Kong for the Trade Fair should be split into reasonable slugs. Nothing too big in one go. Also using a different range of shippers in a staggered timetable. You do this stuff better than I do. This is your business."

"You're right, but it's good to know someone like you agrees with our methodology." Jack grinned.

"One more suggestion," Jens addressed May-Ling. "Perhaps an occasional call to my old friend, Donnie Mullen would be useful. If the merchandise turns up in Hong Kong, with the other facts you've thrown up, maybe his boys'll want to take a closer look. I'll be calling him myself anyway," Kluvin went on. "Donnie knows a thing or two about how these goods get fenced."

"I'm aware of that," said May-Ling as the Chief Inspector rose to leave. "Good advice."

CHAPTER 19

As predicted, Nils Bergman did not appear the next morning.

Throughout that day and Tuesday, Jack and May-Ling continued to work with Hubert Meiss, concentrating on a full reassessment of the entire span of security protocols within Gemtec.

They moved methodically from the top level in the chain of command all the way through to the basic administrative procedures. Their boss, Jules, was a prime believer in getting the tiniest details checked and cross-checked. As in combat, so in running a security organization, the small things counted as much as the large issues.

Word from Kluvin's office gave no encouragement. By Tuesday evening, two days after Bergman's disappearance, no trace of the Volvo surfaced. Checking airline passenger manifests took a long time, with no certainty he went through Schiphol Airport. Searches of the car parks at the airport also came up empty.

Attention turned to lining up the shippers for the consignments for Hong Kong. May-Ling's staff checked out several companies and selected three to undertake the movement of the merchandize. All three had working relationships with parties on the ground in Hong Kong, but no corporate parentage in the colony.

May-Ling ensured ISP double-checked the names through the Companies Registry.

One week later, the first consignments began to arrive at ISP's security vaults in Tsuen Wan, an area at the centre of the primary dockyards in Hong Kong. All of the larger security firms and most of the smaller operators had a presence in the vicinity due to the proximity of the container terminals and loading piers.

May-Ling returned to Hong Kong to be present for the arrival of the initial shipments. Jack insisted in driving her to the airport. As she stepped away into the terminal he knew he'd miss her, an emotion he hadn't experienced for a long time. *Was he getting used to having her around?* Something told him it went deeper, but now he had to get back to work.

Jules and Jack discussed daily the progress on the Gemtec arrangements. Ostman expected things to fall into place quickly. Hubert also got involved on a surface level, but didn't interfere with ISP's direction on choice of shippers. He had general overview of the standards of security but acknowledged the security business logistics were best left with Jack and his people.

The days passed and the continued silence on the fate of Bergman was only of niggling concern to Jack, but Gemtec's chief executive continued to express his worry to Hubert Meiss and to ISP. Jens Kluvin kept his promise to Ostman by calling him every day. The updates routinely showed no fresh information.

A week before the Trade Fair opened, Jack flew to Hong Kong, his first trip to the Far East. Throughout the flight his discomfort was acute as he had to remain strapped to a commercial airliner seat rather than getting poised to fast-land with combat gear and weapons as on countless SAS missions. Somehow, ordinary flying always caused him anxiety. He was not unhappy to hear the whine of the engines taxiing towards the air-bridge.

Since May-Ling's return to Hong Kong, he'd found he'd missed her much more than he'd expected. As with the feelings he'd had at the airport when she left, it was an unfamiliar but comfortable emotion. Although tired from the journey, he anticipated seeing her again.

She waited for him at the arrivals area, after the customs clearance hall. He never travelled with check-in luggage where possible. A hand-carried hold-all did away with the need for waiting at the baggage carousel.

"Good afternoon, Mr Calder. Welcome to my city," May-Ling laughed and kissed his cheek. She looked even more attractive than when he'd sent her off at Schiphol Airport.

"Always encouraging to get firm ground underfoot after hours in the sky," Jack said with some feeling. "You look great. We heading to the office first? I can check into the hotel later, right?" His heart rate pounded like a kid.

"Thanks, you look good yourself. No problem in making Tsuen Wan first stop. I'd like you to eyeball the warehouse arrangements now anyway. There's a lot of value piling up on the Gemtec stuff. And we've got the Thai Jewellery Company's goods in storage too," she said. "One of their consignments is also bound for the Fair."

It took a few minutes to manoeuvre from the lifts to the car park where they collected her vehicle. The black Ford van bore the ISP logo. Jack climbed in the passenger side and threw his hold-all onto the rear seat.

"How far to Tsuen Wan?"

"Not too long in distance, but depending on the time of day it can take twenty minutes or an hour and a half."

Jack soon realized, as with most Chinese drivers in Hong Kong, May-Ling drove like a maniac through traffic. Alternate stampings on the accelerator and brake pedals catapulted them toward Tsuen Wan.

Jack couldn't avoid the visual impact of the Chinese advertising hoardings.

Every shop front competed for eye share. Bright, gaudy colours, strong greens, golds and reds crammed across the streets barely above the level of bus tops, every square inch corralled by some stakeholder or other. Countless boxes and displays with all sorts of goods cluttered the space on the paved sidewalks. A few had English wording and prices, but the majority blazoned in bold Chinese. Pedestrians packed the walkways, often spilling on to the road. Nobody walked slowly. The entire place seemed hell-bent on going somewhere else in a hurry.

Despite the congestion, they took just over half an hour to get to the ISP warehouse. Strong, solid, metal gates defended the front of the building. These opened after three short horn blasts from May-Ling. The gate guard flapped open an eye-grid to ensure the caller's identity before loosening the bolt. The entry to the premises narrowed and led back into a deep hangar with an office area attached to the left-hand side. Inside, several aluminium storage racks and wooden pallets ranged against the walls to facilitate loading and unloading. Two small forklifts and their medium-sized parent operated in the open area in the middle of the warehouse. The hangar accommodated up to six vehicles. There were no windows. Four large air-conditioning units encased with riveted, iron-bar cages jutted through the sides of the building.

Jack liked what he saw. *One way in, the same way out.* Two security cameras scanned the front and back of the area. *No dead scanning coverage.* At the rear, furthest from the door, was the security vault, an armoured walk-in facility eight feet deep, six feet wide and seven feet high. Sufficient for high-value storage goods. Already inside Jack counted at least a dozen of the Gemtec consignment boxes he had supervised on their way out of Amsterdam. *So far, so good.*

Two armed personnel baby-sat the entire area. May-Ling led him into the offices, where a couple of women busied with paperwork. One senior gentleman headed the general administrative duties. They were all Chinese.

"They speak English?" asked Jack.

"Better than you do," retorted May-Ling. "Most of Hong Kong's population is Chinese of some descent or other, but the majority do speak or at least understand English. Most foreigners don't speak more than a few words of Cantonese. All of our staff must be bilingual."

"You double as chief of operations and chief of security?"

"Yes. Until now I've worn both hats, but Jules told me to start interviewing for a chief of security this week. We'll need one for this expanded Gemtec business. By the way, I've invited Donnie Mullen for dinner with us tonight. Okay with you?"

Jack nodded. "Delighted."

"Among the things to discuss with him'll be any ideas he has for security chief candidates."

"What time?"

"Eight o'clock works okay. I'll pick you up at the hotel and we'll treat you to a proper Chinese meal. How does that sound?"

Jack laughed. "No snakes, huh?"

"You wouldn't know whether you were eating snake or not, Jack. Let's get you to your hotel now. It's in downtown Kowloon, overlooking the harbour, handy for the airport and getting back and forward to Tsuen Wan."

"Fine. I could use a good bath. Casual clothing for dinner?"

May-Ling drove to the hotel even more aggressively than in the afternoon. By the time they arrived, Jack reckoned everyone in Hong Kong drove with a death wish.

"See you later," she called, as the wheels screeched away from the kerbside.

CHAPTER 20

No more difficult post exists in the Royal Hong Kong Police Force than Detective Chief Inspector Donnie Mullen's as Head of the Serious Crimes Division.

The call from May-Ling caused Mullen to rerun a few mental tapes.

Old-school, two-fisted cop material, Donnie grew up in the East of Scotland in Dundee but spent his formative career in the London Metropolitan Police Flying Squad heavy crimes unit.

He transferred to Hong Kong in the late seventies to help clean up a corrupt force as well as root out the local bad guys, a tough assignment. Faced with the double-edged threat, Mullen built his own team from scratch and set about the task with gusto.

At times it seemed like the proverbial two steps forward, one step back. Over time, the new breed of police management started to bite successfully. Internal matters became less and less of a concern. A few high-profile arrests of corrupt senior officers from the throw-back era helped to re-establish the much-needed legitimacy of the force. Nicking senior cops from your own squad wasn't easy, but, hey, if these guys couldn't keep themselves straight, no matter how senior and untouchable they considered themselves, they deserved to go down.

Outside of the force, the reach and power of the triads underwent unprecedented growth. For decades, they ran the criminal underworld in Hong Kong in the form of loosely-tied gangs, but by the mid-seventies they had developed into strong, organized groupings. Similar to the Mafia tentacles in the United States, the triad families imposed their criminality on all districts of the colony. Open warfare simmered amongst the different gangs and frequent killings surfaced as retribution for incursions on rival gang territory. Prostitution, drug running, and investments in sleazy bars and clubs provided the primary cash and income sources. Protection rackets squeezed *tong* from small shopkeepers and large businesses alike. Extortion flourished.

Donnie Mullen recalled the summer of 1982 and the day of his promotion to Detective Chief Superintendent, in charge of the Serious Crimes Squad, which also covered triad activities.

"No need to reinvent the wheel," he told his officers. He built several rapid response units along the lines of the Flying Squad. "It worked for us in London, the same'll do here in Hong Kong."

Results came slowly as the tide began to turn. Part of the overt success drove much of the triad blatant activity underground, creating a different kind of problem. It's difficult to fight what can't be seen.

Mullen understood undercover police work would play a more important role in the campaign to neutralize the gangs. A continued annual influx from the United Kingdom allayed some of the constant need to reinforce the corps strength. The salary and living package offered was attractive by England's standards and helped to attract a stream of good quality officers. In 1988, one of these, Ben Marshall, joined Donnie from England. He had a young Chinese wife, May-Ling, serving in the regular police force. An attractive couple and well liked in each of their units, Donnie respected both of them.

Tragedy struck on a sticky, humid, August evening two years later. Ben died in a botched attempt to arrest some members of opposing triad factions in the seedy Mongkok area of Kowloon.

Donnie had no sadder moment in his career than losing one of his best officers but May-Ling lost a husband. To Donnie's astonishment, shortly after Ben's burial, she asked for a move to join the anti-triad unit. He spoke at length with her before finally agreeing to her request. Understanding her motives and her determination, he thought her one of the gutsiest women he had ever met. Within weeks she proposed using her talents as a lead undercover agent and despite the significant risks she insisted on signing up.

A few years later, Jules Townsend needed a reliable, bilingual operative to run a new branch of ISP in Hong Kong and called Donnie Mullen after a referral from their common friend, Jens Kluvin in Amsterdam. Donnie discussed May-Ling with him and recommended Jules

THE VIOLIN MAN'S LEGACY

visit the colony to interview her. He strongly advised her it was time to get out of the police force and into an alternative career. This presented an ideal opportunity for her, he insisted. The need to stay close to Ben's ghost had now been satisfied. She agreed.

The interview with Jules Townsend didn't take long. He made his mind up after only twenty minutes of their discussion over dinner in the Mandarin Hotel Grill Room. She had the right qualities for the job at ISP.

Donnie had maintained constant contact with May-Ling and frequently met her for coffee. He'd been pleased to accept her invitation to dinner with Jack Calder.

* * * * *

Jimmie Chan frowned as he listened to the voice on his secure private telephone.

He thanked the caller for the information and put the receiver back on its cradle. A few seconds later he used the line again to call his brother.

"We seem to have a mosquito problem that needs to be taken care of, Jonnie," he began. The hard, flat-voiced opening customarily signalled a required execution.

"Rotterdam's been pestered with some questions from a woman pretending to be a gems distributor. She really works with a company here in Hong Kong called

International Security Partners. I understand they're involved with Gemtec. You can see the implications, I'm sure."

"Quite so," replied his sibling. "Leave me to deal with it, brother."

CHAPTER 21

The journey to ISP's offices in the afternoon had been an assault on Jack's visual senses. The blur of colours and Chinese script would take a lot of getting used to. Here in Chang's Restaurant, senses of a different kind were under attack.

The noise was overpowering. Children ran and played among the tables. Old people, *really* old people with their extended families gathered round huge circular tables. Waiters in ill-fitting red jackets sprinted from the kitchen to their customers. Orders screamed back and forth through the din, as the floor manageress barked her troops into action. The entire non-stop motion circus fascinated Jack.

Donnie Mullen and May-Ling talked across the bedlam, perfectly in tune with all of this. Jack took some time to adjust his speaking volume to fit in with theirs. Old-style Scottish policemen come in large sizes, cut from the same stock as rugby players and heavyweight boxers. Donnie Mullen stepped straight out of that line, thought Jack. Donnie ordered the food for them in fluent Cantonese.

Jack listened in awe. "How long did you take to learn the lingo?"

The big man answered, "When we arrived in Hong Kong as new cops a six-month crash course came as mandatory, giving us the basics. Thereafter, you're on your own. The best advice I got back then was to find a long-haired dictionary and take her to bed with me." Donnie laughed. "I married my dictionary, and now we've three kids, all boys. Three, seven and twelve. They're fluent in Cantonese as well as English. Calum, my eldest, is captain of his rugby team at the International School. He's better than his father was at his age, I can tell you."

"Sounds good," said Jack, as yet another unrecognizable dish arrived. May-Ling smiled as he tackled the various courses. She warned him to taste a little of each, as one wasn't required finish off everything at a Chinese meal.

An hour passed and other diners dispersed from the tables around them. Their corner table location made conversation without shouting easier. Donnie said something to the waiter and a few minutes later the man brought over a bottle of premium brandy.

The bottle, about a third empty, had a tagged label with Donnie's name. The restaurant was a regular eating hole for the Chief Inspector. Donnie poured three brandies and added ice cubes to the glasses.

"Ice?" Jack asked, surprised.

"The Chinese drink it this way," said May-Ling. "Try."

Jack sipped. "Hmm. Not bad," he said. "An acquired taste, I'm sure, but okay with me."

May-Ling turned the conversation to business. "About a week ago ISP put in applications for firearms licences for Jules, Jack, Malky McGuire and myself, Donnie. This is standard procedure for us in all of our branch locations. We've heard nothing back yet from anyone."

"Don't worry." Donnie lifted his glass. "You'll get them either tomorrow or the day after."

"Thanks," said Jack, butting in. "Can you throw a little light my way on the triad set up, particularly with the Chans, the Half Moon brothers?"

Donnie leant against his chair. "By all means. I gather May-Ling's already begun your local education. Things are starting to change significantly here as Hong Kong's to be returned from the British government to mainland Chinese administration in three years from now." The older man looked serious. "There's a lot of nervousness, particularly among the middle classes. They're scared of what might happen when the Communist regime takes over. Many of them are angling to get green cards and passports for places like the United States, Canada, Australia and England. We've seen a dramatic increase in crime rates in the past couple of years. A last throw of the dice syndrome for many of them. The triads have become even pushier, with their fingers into everything. I suppose they're in a hurry to cash in like everybody else. Some are more dangerous than others."

Jack asked, "How many groups are there?"

"Thirty to forty. Only seven or eight are serious criminal outfits. They hold by far the biggest membership. The smallest have hundreds in their gangs, the largest perhaps thousands. Not all the gang members are up for the big-time crime, lots just like the buzz of being associated."

Jack nodded and glanced at May-Ling, sure she knew this already. "Pretty much the flies to the bright light, huh?"

"Correct. The Half Moon boys are heavy-duty bad news. Involved in just about every nasty angle you can imagine, but slippery as hell. Their lawyers earn their money. We haven't been able to lay as much as a finger near them in the twenty years since I've been here. It would be a real score to put them away." May-Ling lowered her glass, also nodding agreement with Donnie.

"Does no-one ever see them?" asked Jack.

"On the contrary," countered the policeman. "They lead pretty open lives. Their businesses run, on the surface, within the law. We track them regularly of course. Even though we can't pin them directly, we keep tabs on where they are. For example, Jonnie Half Moon has a regular late Wednesday night tryst with a European hooker. She's picked up from one of the high-class escort clubs in Kowloon around nine o'clock and taken over to Wong Tai Sin to the Heavenly Clouds Motel."

Jack raised his eyebrows in disbelief. "Motel? In Hong Kong? Who needs one here? No-one drives any further than ten miles."

"Quite so," responded May-Ling, with a smile. "Motels rent their rooms by the hour. Some are kitted out with fantasy features, signature rooms, mirrored ceilings, spas, water beds. It's a flourishing industry. Few self-respecting Chinese businessmen *don't* maintain mistresses, plural."

"Oh," said Jack, his education being updated by the second.

"Jonnie's on the dot every Wednesday night, and for the last six months, the same lady partner." Donnie told him. "She's from Manchester. Works in the club, so we can't do her for outright prostitution. His brother also follows a regular Wednesday night routine."

"Also at a motel?"

"No. Even more Chinese in style. Jimmie hosts a mahjong evening at his villa out in the country in Sai Kung. Hong Kong holds plenty of countryside for its size, especially up toward the border. He invites seven Wednesday players, making up two mahjong tables. All high-class thugs in my opinion," Donnie added. "I'll guarantee every cent they gamble is money stolen from somebody else. He always keeps a couple of bodyguards with him, one of whom has form. We sent him down for five years when I first got here. He was wheel-man for a jewellery store smash and grab in the centre of Hong Kong in the middle of the day. Lucky for him we picked him up with no weapons aboard or he'd still be in jail."

"What's the whisper on the street about the gems stolen in Amsterdam turning up here?" asked May-Ling, changing the subject.

Donnie poured another drink. "Pretty reliable. You know as well as I do, sometimes we can discount a whisper and other times we think we should listen."

May-Ling added more ice to her brandy glass. "Right," she said.

"Now here's what you *really* need to hear," Donnie carried on. "Another tickle has come in, involving you guys. Or more specifically your Gemtec goods for the Trade Fair."

Jack and May-Ling looked at each other. Jack lowered his glass. "Go on. What's the whisper?"

"The word is you'll be moving upwards of twelve million US dollars worth of merchandize, enough to catch the attention of the bad guys. And from me. I'll be in sync with what you're doing as your stuff gets moved. I'm prepared to let some of my people accompany it. I don't want that kind of value to disappear on my patch. Nor do I need any innocent citizens taken out in a Chinese shoot-out." Donnie had lowered his voice.

Jack replied. "We'd welcome having your boys ride shotgun with us, and of course, we'd be prepared to pay whatever costs you think appropriate. The amount *is* large. I'm not surprised it's getting some focus. I told Jules I also want my partner, Malky McGuire, over here for the next week while the goods are in Hong Kong. He's arriving mid-day tomorrow. I intend to map out how and when we move the stuff over to the Trade Fair at the Hong Kong Coliseum. Can I sit with you in a day or two to work through the details?"

Donnie nodded. "Sure."

"Do you think it's the Half Moon people?" Jack asked him.

"Could be, which means the Ching Tan Ka triads. Or maybe the Mok Kwong Cho. A lot of friction's been building between them in the last few months. They're the two most likely candidates, but regardless of which, when the other gets wind of it, a turf battle's likely brewing," explained Mullen.

"Understood."

The bill arrived and Jack noticed May-Ling took it from the waiter. Mullen didn't argue. Jack was beginning to see another, assertive side to his Chinese partner. She was one smart, tough lady. And this was her patch.

CHAPTER 22

Mullen eased into the rear of his police Rover and Jack took the passenger seat in May-Ling's Toyota.

She suggested they swing by her flat for a nightcap rather than go straight back to drop him at the Shangri-La. He didn't need much persuasion. He *had* missed her company in the week after she returned to Hong Kong. Her wild driving was tempered in the lighter, late-night traffic.

The block of flats where she lived in Beacon Hill in Kowloon Tong replicated a multitude of similar buildings in a city which had developed upward rather than outward. Neither ugly nor pretty, for May-Ling the spacious accommodation was close to her office. The combination would have satisfied most of the population in Hong Kong.

May-Ling parked the car near to the block and approached the front entrance. They entered the foyer and Jack spotted the caretaker behind a metal table in the corner. He was a small Chinese, of indeterminate age, but certainly much older than Jack.

The man sidled from behind the table and quickly disappeared through an opening into a corridor at the side of the hallway, which in itself didn't disturb Jack. The scared look in the man's eyes as he turned away *did* catch his attention. Adrenaline shot through Jack's body as his instincts kicked into overdrive.

They moved towards the lift and Jack closed a hand around May-Ling's elbow. He asked, "What floor?"

"Four."

"Hit seven instead," he ordered.

"Why?"

"Trust me. Just hit seven."

May-Ling pressed the button for the seventh.

Jack put his finger to his lips to signal silence as they stepped out slowly. The open staircase led up the side of the lift bank. Nobody else appeared. In single file, they quietly eased downstairs in the almost quarter-light. Jack took a few seconds to adjust his vision to the difference in the darker area. May-Ling followed several feet behind him. Halfway down from the fifth to the fourth floor Jack saw him, a dark-clothed man, shoulder-length hair, one hand cupping a cigarette, the other inside the fold of his jacket, leaning against the wall. He was hidden in the shadows, captured by a glimmer of light from across the stairwell opening.

Jack moved swiftly but the slight sound of his feet on the gravelly surface of the backstairs caused the man to crouch. The cigarette flicked to the ground. A stiletto flashed from inside the man's jacket. He ran towards Jack with the blade lunging in front of him. This one was easy.

A simple body movement took the thrusting arm a little beyond Jack. In one motion, Jack looped an arm around the throat, stepped back with the thug in a deadlock and twisted upward and sideway using the leverage of the man's chin against his own weight. The neck snapped with the sound of a dry twig breaking underfoot. The intruder's body went limp and Jack let him slip to the ground on top of the cigarette.

So much for a frontal stab attack. Idiot.

He became conscious of another noise. A second assailant ran from the other side of the landing, also with a knife pointed toward him. Jack braced ready to receive the impact. It never came. Instead, a flurry of movement intercepted the man's rush. May-Ling reached under the outstretched arm and levered in the classic dis-arm technique. The man squealed as his fingers released the weapon. The knife slid from his hand and May-Ling caught the handle, spinning the man to face her. With her nose almost touching the attacker's, she drove the steel upward under the left rib cage and turned it hard. He died in seconds as the metal blade ruptured his heart. Like his partner, he slid noiselessly to the landing floor.

Jack stared, motionless for a moment.

Where the hell did she learn that?

"You okay?" he asked at last. "I'm impressed, Miss Wong. I'm learning more about you every day."

"Ben and I met during a series of martial arts and combat courses in London," she shrugged, hardly out of breath. "It's often come in handy."

Jack grinned, realising why Jules Townsend had considered May-Ling such a powerful candidate to join ISP. He stepped toward her and embraced her in a warm hug knowing they had just shared a real moment together, a moment in which either one or both of them could have been injured or killed.

Donnie Mullen took the call from Jack, who briefed him on what had happened. "I'll be there in ten minutes," said the policeman.

By the time Donnie arrived at May-Ling's apartment with three other plainclothes officers, she had prepared coffee. Jack noted the obvious respect from her former colleagues as they greeted her.

Donnie spoke. "These are low-life triad soldiers, Jack. The tattoos tell us they're from the Ching Tan Ka, the Half Moons' organization. The clowns wear the things like badges. Don't worry about the stiffs. We'll make them vanish. The serious point is May-Ling was the target." He looked from her to Jack. "It doesn't take a genius to figure out they've made the connection between the calls in Amsterdam and who she really represents. This ties in with what you and Jens told me about Nils Bergman's disappearance. The Half Moons are clever boys, Jack. At this point, I still don't have enough to go chase them down. Unfortunately, neither does Jens, who'd love to go rip their offices apart in Amsterdam and Rotterdam. We're dealing with a delicate situation."

A rush of concern hit Jack as he realised May-Ling had been tonight's target, and taking out the two attackers didn't remove the danger she clearly faced now, "We can't have May-Ling exposed like this, Donnie. I'm also worried about a possible attack on ISP's operations in Tsuen Wan. We've other employees to think of, too. I'll double the armed guards at the warehouse. For tonight and for the next few days, May-Ling can billet at the hotel where I can keep an eye on her, although from what I saw earlier, she's pretty handy at looking after herself."

Jack gave her a swift smile.

"I agree," said Donnie. "No point in having too many places to cover until we can get a better grip on this. I reckon after the Gemtec merchandize returns to Holland, the heat'll die down. Let's talk in the morning on your plans for the next few days."

"Can we meet early evening instead?" asked May-Ling. "Malky arrives at mid-day. He should be with us when we go over this stuff."

"Fine. Seven o'clock at the hotel?"

"Ok," agreed Jack. "Pack a bag, May-Ling and let's get you a room at the Shangri La."

* * * * *

Neither of them spoke on the drive to the hotel, but his concern for her well-being stoked emotions of care long dormant in him. After leaving the Toyota to be valet-parked they walked across the lobby toward the check-in desk. On the spur of the moment he turned to her to speak and she also began to talk. Like two confused kids, they laughed. "Yes, Jack?"

"I wonder if you'd be safer sharing my room with me. I can sleep on the couch in there. I'd be more relaxed about you."

"I'm way ahead of you, Jack. I'd already decided I'll be in your room, but if you think I'll be alone in your bed, you're crazy. If I'm mistaken, tell me so, but I think you've been thinking what I've been feeling for a while now."

"You mean, we'll sleep together?" he said, realizing how clumsy he sounded.

She smiled slowly at him. "Mr Calder. It would be highly impolite of me to refuse such a generous offer. It's already late, don't you think we should be in by bed now?"

The elevator journey to his room took only minutes and Jack wondered if he was out of line. *She's still a colleague, for Christ's sake. What was the old saying, 'Never take your meat where you make your bread'? God, what kind of a daft bastard am I?*

May-Ling showed no signs of second thoughts. With purposeful strides she reached the door and turned to wait for him. He inserted the key and the lock clicked open.

Jack stammered, "Are you sure you...?"

She grasped his wrist in reply and pulled him into the room. With her back against the door, she put both hands behind his head and brought her lips up to meet his. Hungry mouths took over. Reserve vanished as their bodies tangled in the way only violent lust can deliver. He ripped away her blouse and bra and she deftly undid his belt, sliding his pants to the carpet.

"Take me, Jack! Take me now!" she urged. He pulled her skirt upward, garlanding her naked waist. He thrust inside her with an urgency long forgotten. They lowered as one to the carpet, her legs clasped behind his hips. She felt the roughness of the carpet on her buttocks as he drove harder and harder into her.

"Yes, Jack! Yes!"

They climaxed together, neither aware of anything but the shudder in their loins.

May-Ling recovered her breath and spoke first. "My God. That was amazing, Mr Calder. You wanna try the bed this time?"

A couple of hours later, they drifted off to sleep, arms and legs loosely draped around each other. Sometime in the middle of the night, May-Ling became conscious of her sleeping partner's restlessness. Jack was not awake, but his body shook and what passed as stifled yells came from his mouth. Nightmare. She made out the slurring of the name 'Roddie' a couple of times, along with a murmured

'Violin Man'. She remembered her own episodes of similar bad dreams. The shooting of Ben took several months back then to exorcise from her sleep. She huddled closer to Jack, and softly embraced him, caressing his forehead until his body relaxed. Still entangled when the dawn broke, this time their lovemaking was much gentler.

CHAPTER 23

Deborah Devlin was a stunning head-turner. At just under six feet tall, her presence in a room guaranteed attention from both men and women, the latter with a good deal of envy.

In her mid-twenties now, Deborah's physical attributes more than adequately compensated her lack of success in school. A brief career in an office role in Manchester gave way to a series of shop assistant jobs in supermarkets and ladies' garment stores. The discotheque party and nightclub scene became a natural playground for her, with never a lack of boyfriends. A bubbly personality and innate confidence guaranteed lots of invitations.

She acquired the nickname, Double-D Debbie, not so much for her initials, more as a pointer to her body measurements. She took the label in her stride with great humour. If you've got it flaunt it, she'd say. She liked a drink, but never indulged the endless offers of soft and hard drugs plaguing the clubs in all the big cities.

A friend introduced Debbie to the shadowy world of escort services as a means of picking up easy money. Her first assignment was a German company executive who wanted to get her into bed the minute they met. She made an awkward excuse and left the man after only ten minutes.

"I can't do this," she insisted to the girlfriend who'd brought her to the agency. "I don't think I'm cut out for it." Her friend persisted and they tried a double date the next evening. This turned out more straight-forward than the first night. She also liked the guy and willingly split to go to his bedroom.

Earnings from the escort business soon outmatched anything she could ever make from her day jobs. A rapidly-growing clientele base translated to a regular income much superior to the pay checks her ex-school girl friends earned in professional careers.

The lure of travel brought Debbie and her friend to Hong Kong. The intended ten-day vacation eased into a protracted stay, the nightlife even busier than Manchester, she realized. The local escort agencies afforded ample and lucrative access to another set of clients in the colony. In exchange for four nights per week committed work in a high-class lounge night club in Kowloon, her employers arranged a permanent work permit. Most of the club's customers were out-of-town visiting executives with generous entertainment expenses, looking for a bit of glamour to fill the evenings with their new business partners. Debbie found her lifestyle much better than in England.

The club entertained all sorts of nationalities, with the implicit understanding for the right price the ladies made themselves available for extra, more intimate services away from the premises. Debbie received countless offers.

At first, she was unaware the Chinese businessman who began to take a close interest in her owned the club.

Jonnie Chan, polite and charming in open company, always immaculately dressed, spoke perfect English. Unmarried, he had a string of female friends for his night-time companionship. She thought the red crescent birthmark on his temple looked cute.

After three or four one-night stands with him, she agreed to spend a few hours with Jonnie every Wednesday evening. Generous with money, he also gave her expensive personal gifts of jewellery or perfume. By no means a love affair, the business arrangement suited both of them.

He had his personal sexual-play peccadilloes, verging on what the escort fraternity alluded to as 'rough trade', given and received. This, she found, fitted well with her own bedroom preferences, to a degree. Debbie relished the sessions, not bad getting paid for doing something she enjoyed. When she explained her Double-D tag to Jonnie, he laughed and called her his 'Debble-Debbie'.

The routine had her picked up at nine o'clock prompt from the club. No dinner. No fancy frills. Straight to the Heavenly Cloud Motel. Jonnie always had a glass of brandy poured, waiting for her to arrive. The initial couple of times were fun, but after a while, Jonnie's behaviour grew more violent. He regularly left marks on her body, on parts not visible when she dressed. Inflicting more pain than necessary became his high. Despite her pleadings to ease up, this spurred him to increased malevolence. By now, she also understood the darker side of his business, and was scared to resist too much. Rumours of other girls disappearing from the club worried the hell out of her.

Their trysts took a couple of hours at most, after which Jonnie's driver returned her to the club. Her lover always remained behind. Unknown to Debbie, every Wednesday around midnight, another regular followed her sessions. The second visitor for Jonnie Half Moon was a black, lady-boy from Brazil, the transvestite also unaware Debbie had preceded him. Even Donnie Mullen's Anti-Triad team had no knowledge of this additional line of play by the Chinese triad boss.

Debbie took stock. Six months they'd been at it, her bank balance pretty healthy, with far more brass than she could have stashed back home, but she sensed this game had a limited shelf-life. Mom had always preached the need to put the pennies away for the future. Time to do a runner? She had enough money now to get a place for herself in London or back in Manchester. She wouldn't have to do any of this stuff for a couple of years at least. Apart from this violence shit from Jonnie, life is good. How to make the break without pissing him off? Debbie frowned. No use having a pile in the bank if you were parked in a grave…

CHAPTER 24

Jack had talked to Malky McGuire on the phone daily since the move to Amsterdam a month earlier. He looked forward to catching up with his partner again in person.

This first big assignment with Gemtec meant a great deal to Jules and the whole company. The next few days in Hong Kong demanded a lot of care and attention. He welcomed the offer of cooperation from Donnie Mullen but nothing beat having McGuire on watch, no better man to have around than the Irishman. Jack and he had been constant buddies since joining the SAS on the same day. A touch under six feet, slightly shorter than Jack, Malky packed a muscle-bound farming son's body into his uniform. His self-deprecating manner belied a brain as sharp as any Jack had ever met, coupled with a quiet sense of humour.

The slices of humanity Malky encountered right from the start of his military career made all his home country's religious bigotry a far-faded nonsense. His platoon buddies cared nothing for religious differences, solid mates regardless of which side of the divide they were born into. As the saying went, the wider world became his oyster.

Malky first served across the globe with the Irish Guards, including a stint as part of the British Garrison at Stanley Fort in Hong Kong in 1971. He enjoyed his tours of duty. He stepped up to the SAS in 1974. Now, more than twenty years later, for the first time since he sailed out of Hong Kong in 1972, he was flying back in. This time, to join his buddy, Jack Calder. He emerged from the arrivals exit at Kai Tak Airport and the bear-hug between them said it all.

CHAPTER 25

DCI Mullen brought his number two with him to the seven o'clock meeting. Detective Inspector Archie Campbell, another Scot, arrived in Hong Kong around the same time as Mullen. They'd operated together for twenty years, and their record as a successful team was unparalleled. Archie was as slim as Donnie was stocky and large; quiet where his mate was gregarious; both shared a pugnacious tenacity in cleaning out criminals. May-Ling reserved a private meeting room in the hotel business centre.

Malky had run his professional eye over Tsuen Wan during the day in a similar manner to Jack's earlier review. He reinforced the approval of the arrangements at the ISP warehouse, including the additional manned guards. Now for the coordination with the local cops. The greetings formalities over, Jack moved to outline the plan to move the jewellery and gems from the security vault to the Hong Kong Coliseum.

"You taking it all in one shot, or in parts?" Donnie Mullen posed the first question.

"One run, one shift."

"Value?"

"Your street word was near the mark. Twelve and a half million dollars worth."

"That's kind of heavy to have hanging around the streets of Hong Kong for too long," interjected Archie Campbell. "You sure you don't want to shift smaller bites?"

Jack replied, "The distance is quite short. I'd rather move in one go. We've done the routes a few times now. There's two alternatives. One is through the inner road along the West Kowloon corridor. The other is the harbour route along the West Kowloon Highway. Neither is much more than about eight miles in all."

"So which way are you going to go?" asked Archie.

"We'll take the harbour road, but I want you to tell your street whisperers we're using the inner route."

"Nice one," said Donnie. "And timing?"

"Early Friday morning," broke in May-Ling. "At two o'clock sharp. There should be minimal traffic. "We reckon passage time of no more than twenty to twenty-five minutes. Guards at the Hong Kong Coliseum are on duty round the clock, so no need to inform them when we're coming."

"The only others in the know apart from the five of us will be Deryk Ostman and Hubert Meiss. Let's see how effective your street narks are," added Jack.

"I think you can rest assured word'll get back to the bad guys quickly enough," said Archie. "What about transportation and escorts?"

Malky answered. "We'll use two vans, the first one with Jack, myself, May-Ling and a driver. We thought your boys would take the second van in back-up position. This is our merchandize after all."

"May-Ling is going too?" Donnie asked, with a tinge of surprise in his voice.

"Yes," came the Chinese lady's emphatic reply.

Donnie stared at her for a moment, pursed his lips and shrugged. "Okay. It's your show, guys."

Archie Campbell spoke. "What kind of firepower you carrying?"

"MP5s," replied Malky.

"We'll have the same," said Donnie.

"We?" queried Jack, with a slight frown.

"Your back-up'll be Archie and I, and two of my best guys with a driver. I said before, I don't need any innocent take-downs on my patch."

"Appreciated. So everybody wants to be at the party, huh?" jested Jack. "We've got Kevlar bullet-proof vests for a little added insurance. You want some?"

"We have those too," smiled Donnie. "Wouldn't feel properly dressed without them."

"Anything else we need to cover?" asked May-Ling.

"Nope, I think we keep things simple and pray for a smooth ride Friday morning," said Archie, reaching out to shake hands with each of them. "We'll be here about an hour before the trip."

"Goodnight all," his superior officer added as they made for the door.

CHAPTER 26

Earlier the same day in Amsterdam, six hours time difference away, Jens Kluvin and his squad got the first real piece of luck all detectives pray for in a difficult case.

Since the disappearance of Nils Bergman, there'd been no trace of the man, nor of his Volvo. Continued enquiries at the airline offices in Schiphol yielded nothing. As a routine procedure, Kluvin had ordered a daily check of the Norwegian's mailbox at his residential block. Now, almost two weeks after he'd vanished, an additional piece of mail addressed to Bergman joined the usual junk flyers and utility bills.

The expensive, higher-grade envelope bore the sender's elegantly embossed name, Banque Wilhelm & Roche, Private Bankers, Amsterdam.

"Kinda high-class paper. High-class bankers. Let's see what Mr Nils tucked away," murmured the Chief.

Dick de Jong and Jens Kluvin opened it together in the Chief Inspector's office. They had no official authorization to open mail without a warrant, but Jens decided he would attend to that detail at a later date. The envelope contained several account statement sheets and an elaborate, hand-written note embellished above the printed name of the writer. The signature proclaimed the manager of Banque Wilhelm & Roche. The content of Bergman's account statement held riveting information.

Gemtec's absentee head of operations and logistics seemed to have a means of income other than his salary from the gem company. The starting balance showed a staggering two million, three hundred and seventy thousand dollars. Four days prior to his disappearance a further credit lodged in the account amounting to two hundred thousand dollars. The ream of statement sheets recorded a steady accrual over two or three years.

"However good an administrator for Gemtec, he didn't make that kind of money shoving logistics schedules around," ventured de Jong.

"Hmmm," replied his boss. "Looks like the credits began about three years ago, after he'd been with Ostman and Meiss for a year. Worth checking with Ostman if they're missing that much in goods over the period."

The following entries were equally interesting. On the date after receipt of the last inward payment the account recorded two withdrawals, the first for sixty-five thousand dollars, the second for an amount of two million five hundred thousand dollars. The balance in the account had reduced to only five thousand dollars.

Jens Kluvin decided he and de Jong should visit the bank manager. The compliment slip carried the direct telephone line of the signatory. Jens introduced himself and explained the reason for his call. He apologized for the short notice but the executive agreed that assisting Chief Inspector Kluvin in the pursuit of enquiries regarding Mr Nils Bergman would not be amiss.

"Thank you, sir. We'll be with you in about half an hour. I trust we won't take up much of your time."

Thank God the bank wasn't in Switzerland.

Jens Kluvin had had occasion in the past to visit elegant bank offices such as these of Banque Wilhelm & Roche. Sometimes he had to carry the all-sweeping court warrant with him, as some bankers refused to speak to police without authorized documentation. By the tone of the bank officer's voice on the telephone, Jens surmised this gentleman wouldn't need such legalities.

Discretion is a comfortable mantle worn by private banks. Client confidentiality being paramount, at no point in the passage into or out of Banque Wilhelm & Roche's premises would visitors meet any person other than bank personnel. Closed circuit cameras monitored and piloted guests through the heavily-carpeted corridors to private salons. Each salon had two doors. The bank officer meeting his or her visitor would arrive moments before the client. Mahogany chairs embracing a leather-bound desk replicated in every private reception room.

From his telephone conversation, Kluvin had somehow expected a small gentleman, but instead the man stood taller than himself, and bore an extended girth. He carried a thin, buff-coloured folder, tucked neatly under his left elbow. He came straight to the point.

"Good day, Chief Inspector. I'm the branch manager

here. You enquired about a Mr Bergman. How may I assist you?"

"Good afternoon, sir," replied Jens Kluvin, respectfully. "This is my deputy, Detective Inspector de Jong. I'm grateful for your time, particularly at such short notice. As I explained to you over the phone, I head the Serious Crimes Division headquartered here in Amsterdam. We have reason to believe your client, Nils Bergman may be involved in the execution of at least two recent robberies involving the deaths of three citizens. We understand from a document which has come into our possession an account in his name with your bank has been the subject of unusually large dollar transfers in the last couple of weeks. It is vital to our investigation to trace the origin of these funds and where the final amounts have been sent."

Jens paused while the other man digested this information, before continuing. "Sir, I won't pretend I have a formal warrant to request this of you, but I assure you I can have it within the day if necessary. I further guarantee in no way would I seek to cause any awkwardness or embarrassment for your esteemed bank."

The manager greeted Kluvin's statement with a nod. He placed the unmarked folder on the desk in front of him and pushed it closer to the Chief Inspector.

"Sir, we at Banque Wilhelm & Roche would always seek to cooperate with our friends in the police. However, you do appreciate I can't disclose to you information of a confidential nature about clients of this bank without the proper authority to do so. Indeed, I'm not even permitted to confirm or deny any such account in the name you've mentioned."

"Yes, sir." Jens waited.

The executive spoke quietly. "Chief Inspector, it seems my presence is required elsewhere in the bank right now. I must leave you and Mr de Jong alone in this room until I'm able to return, which will be in about twenty minutes. We may resume our conversation when I get back."

The man stared Jens Kluvin straight in the eye and pushed the folder even closer to the policeman across the desk. He then excused himself and closed the door behind him as he exited the room.

"Old school, Dick. Always the best," chuckled Jens. "Let's get some reading done."

* * * * *

The history of receipts into the account verified a steady flow of funds going back for more than three and a half years. The amounts differed on each remittance. The similarity, which soon became obvious, appeared in the common tag name of the senders, most of them companies with the title 'Fortune' in them. Initiated from offshore banks in the British Virgin Islands, Channel Islands, and the Dutch Antilles. Jens nodded. All subsidiaries of the

Fortune Holdings Group in Hong Kong, the same outfit May-Ling had uncovered.

This constituted cause enough to pull search warrants for Pan Asia and Allied Trading and the people running these companies, including Messrs Kai and Choi.

This was better. The Half Moons' smart finance guys had slipped up here, big time. It would still be tricky to prove a direct tie-in to the Chans, but at least Jens and his team could put the local operators out of commission, and get Donnie Mullen to probe the Hong Kong end. Now, where had Bergman remitted the funds in the last two weeks?

The covering instruction documents held explicit details. The sixty-five thousand dollars payment channelled to a company account in a bank in Chile. Sent through Banco Bice in Santiago, for onward remittance to Banco Bice in San Pedro de Atacama. Kluvin would check an atlas when they got back to headquarters.

The second payment for two million, five hundred thousand dollars, favoured a joint account at Banco Credito Primera in La Paz, Bolivia. The names on the account were unfamiliar to the detectives. One was Philip Jacoob, the other John Vogel.

"Interesting," said Kluvin, while Dick de Jong continued scribbling in his notebook. "Either Bergman has accomplices, or two aliases."

"Maybe. Better finish now before our friend returns. I think we've covered it all," replied his deputy, as he folded his pad and stuck it back into his coat pocket.

Jens replaced the closed file on the desk in front of them. Right on cue, the bank manager entered the room once more. He offered his hand and said, "Gentlemen, I'm sorry not to have been able to help you further. Please call me if there's anything Banque Wilhelm & Roche can assist you with in the future."

The policemen got to their feet. "Indeed, sir. I'm grateful to you. Thanks for your assistance," replied Jens.

On the way back to their office, they discussed the information contained in de Jong's notes.

"I doubt very much our Mr Bergman came to any mortal harm," opened Jens. "This tells me he's comfortably away in South America. Have the sniffers check the airlines passenger lists for recent flights to Chile and see if his name appears. At least it would help focus on where he headed."

"Yes, maybe a bit of light at last," said de Jong.

"Also, contact May-Ling in Hong Kong with the names of these other 'Fortune' companies. Ask her to check if they're part of the group she traced already. Let's take nothing for granted. Another day or two at this stage won't make any difference, so long as we nail them. Remember, if the Chan twins' outfit is involved in this, they use tons of lawyers. When we do hit them, let's ensure the case sticks like a leech."

"Understood, boss. What about Choi and Kai and the companies here in Holland?" asked de Jong.

"Same thing. We'll need positive confirmations before we move. Line up the warrants but hold fire until we cross-check the Hong Kong connections."

"And the banks in Chile and Bolivia? What chance of the local boys there helping out?"

Kluvin grimaced. "My experience with them in the past isn't good. I hate to say, but money still talks in their part of the world. It's difficult to get these guys excited about other forces' problems. No harm in trying, though. Send them the details and ask for whatever help they can give us. We might be lucky again, but I think it's pushing our chances. Oh, and check out where we'll find San Pedro de Atacama. I bet you there's a hundred towns called San Pedro in Chile."

As Jens got out of the car, he had the feeling perhaps at last they were getting somewhere.

CHAPTER 27

The sequence run-through for the early Friday morning delivery to the Hong Kong Coliseum took up much of Wednesday in Tsuen Wan.

Jack, Malky and May-Ling allowed nobody apart from themselves to enter the security vault area. They repeated the familiar, comprehensive, pre-operations schedule, all done out of sight of others in the warehouse; the armoured vans to be used on the night inspected to ensure that no mechanical hiccup would impede the journey; the MP5s also checked several times; the same for the bullet-proof vests. May-Ling observed Malky and Jack at ease with the weapons in their hands. They rehearsed over and over the specific action procedures they'd follow if an attack happened.

Detail, detail, detail.

Towards the end of the afternoon, everything was ready. Jack locked the vault containing the arms and the merchandize and returned to the office. May-Ling had just finished a call to Archie Campbell.

"Archie says the word has been put out and already a different whisperer has brought it back as street news," she said.

"Fine," replied Malky. "If anybody comes to the party, we'll be ready to welcome them."

May-Ling sensed these guys almost hoped there would be an attempt on them.

"Not much more to do now," said Jack. "You fancy dinner?" Jack was perpetually hungry in the run-up to potential combat action.

"Why not?" said Malky. "May-Ling, how about a real Chinese meal? I haven't had a good one of those since I left Hong Kong twenty years ago."

"No problem," she responded. "Let's go down to Kowloon Tong and eat some proper stuff in a local restaurant, not the fancy tourist garbage."

Both men smiled.

* * * * *

Unlike Chang's on the Monday evening, this place didn't even have a name. Rough, service tables surrounded the eatery, open on three sides. Neither man sighted a menu.

May-Ling did the ordering this time, with a lot of pointing toward various food items hanging from spikes near the cooking stoves. The noise in the kitchen area equalled the racket from Chang's as the cooks competed with each other in the decibel stakes.

A varied assortment of dishes began to arrive. A large bowl with cooked rice was placed in the centre of the table, which the waiter refilled any time it got close to being empty. Scalding hot Chinese tea was dispensed in straight glasses with no handles. It took Jack a while to get used to holding these at the rim to avoid burning his fingers.

A succession of dishes ferried from the kitchen to their table, none of which he could name, but Malky certainly could. Deep-fried prawn fritters; diced chicken in a dark, oyster sauce; duck strips in a heavy, carmelized dressing; pork sliced in sesame, capped with a mixture of herbs and spices; and enough steamed rice and noodles to sink a battleship. The Irishman was in his element. "Man, I haven't eaten this well for a hundred years," he said, licking some sauce from his thumb. "We used to get out once a week at Stanley Market and murder this stuff. Even on a soldier's pay, we had change left at the end."

Jack watched his partner tackle each plate as if he hadn't fed for a month.

With Malky around, he knew this week would work out well. In turn, Malky recognized the quiet, thinking mode Jack always adopted before field-work. The pair had worked together almost by telepathy in over two dozen combat arenas around the world.

Malky also liked Jack's positive reaction to May-Ling. His pal was more relaxed than he'd seen in several months. She's good for him, he thought.

With serious business due in just over twenty-four hours they drank only Chinese tea, poured from a never-empty pot. No alcohol. May-Ling showed Jack how to use chopsticks, which to his surprise he mastered in a few minutes.

They spent a couple of hours over dinner until time to leave. Malky offered to pay, but as he had no local money, Jack pushed several notes on to the table, including a generous tip.

The evening air was balmy rather than humid.

"Let's walk a bit," suggested May-Ling. "There's a street bazaar along here you might find fun." She chain-linked arms with her two colleagues and they strolled toward the market about a hundred yards down from the restaurant. Rows and rows of stalls spread out, with makeshift lighting from fluorescent tubes dangled across the front of each one, displaying silver trinkets, wood carvings, silk scarves, umpteen displays of gold necklets and bangles, ties and sports shirts and all sorts of oddments. Nothing had price tags. The hawkers barraged the ears of anyone in range of their lungs. They hollered in Cantonese and in pidgin English when they saw the two Europeans with the Chinese lady.

May-Ling stopped at a stall with an array of jade products. The grey-haired seller began an animated conversation with her in a bargaining battle. May-Ling waved her hand dismissively and made to walk away. The woman called her back, almost pleading with her. They exchanged a few more short sentences until a final clapping of the hands from the older woman signalled the end of the bartering. They had reached agreement. Jack was fascinated.

From May-Ling's handbag a clutch of banknotes appeared. She talked in Cantonese as she gave the money to the woman, both of them all smiles. She picked up two pieces of dark-green jade and handed one each to Jack and Malky.

"What's this?" asked Jack.

"For luck, Mr Calder and Mr McGuire. We Chinese are supposed to be superstitious people. Didn't anyone ever tell you?"

Jack knew she was using that as an excuse to give them a present. On her turf in Hong Kong, her way of saying welcome. Both men gave profuse thanks and kissed her on the cheek.

"Wait." said Jack. He approached the old woman and pointed to another piece of jade. "How much?"

"Seven hundred Hong Kong dollars," came the reply.

"Too much, too much," said Jack, trying to copy the bartering skills of May-Ling.

"Okay, Mister. Special for you, for beautiful lady, six hundred fifty."

"Six hundred," he countered, enjoying the exchange.

"Oh you, Mister. You tough man. Six hundred thirty, and everybody make happy." A toothy, gold smile beamed at him.

He laughed. "Okay, everybody make happy. Six hundred thirty. Here, keep the change." He gave the old lady a thousand Hong Kong dollar bill. So much for bartering.

The jade piece was translucent. Malky and May-Ling giggled too.

Jack approached May-Ling with the gift held out in his hand.

"Miss Wong. A beautiful piece for a beautiful lady. The seller said so, therefore she must be right. We Scots are also supposed to be superstitious. Didn't anybody ever tell you?" and he handed the stone to May-Ling.

"Thank you, Mr Calder." She kissed him.

Malky grinned. "We Irish are supposed to be superstitious as well, but not daft enough to buy things for the whole world the way the Scots do." They all roared with laughter.

They started walking again before May-Ling stopped them once more a few yards along the street.

"Look," she pointed to a sign in the alleyway. "A fortune-teller. Come on Jack. Let's get your fortune told."

"Not for me, I don't need my future told. Like reading your stars in the tea-leaves. I'll leave that to you and the Irish leprechaun."

"Oh, come on Jack. It's a bit of fun," she insisted, taking his hand and tugging him towards the doorway.

"Alright. But no tea-leaves, okay?"

* * * * *

The tiny room just about held them all. Inside, shadowy, dim light diffused from a heavy, red lampshade with brocaded gold and green trimmings. Ornate, brown, wooden carvings hung from brass hooks around the walls, representing figures of various half-animal, half-human forms. The chairs, in contrast, were of simple, light-coloured bamboo, with thick cushions, also in deep, red cloth. The air filled with the aroma from the smoking joss sticks, a mixture of at least two different incense smells. A narrow table covered in green baize held time-yellowed jotters fronted with Chinese lettering. Jack's gaze drew past the table to the figure seated on the other side.

The fortune-teller reminded him of old, sepia pictures of dateless, Chinese patriarchs. The man must have been at least eighty. His skull was completely bald on top, with silvered, thin wisps of hair starting from the sides of his ears, journeying down and across his jowls, meeting to continue as extended mustachios down to the middle of his chest. The eyebrows tufted upwards to complete the corral of silver around his face. His skin texture resembled the pages of old books found in museums. But the eyes magnetized Jack. Piercing, dark pools, with a hint of white fleck in the left, confirmed a gentleman of some veneration. The trio sat down and May-Ling offered a salutation in Cantonese. The fortune-teller blinked his eyes slowly and nodded his head gently towards them. He returned her greeting in a husky tone. They conversed a little further. May-Ling addressed Jack.

"He wants you to tell him the month and year you were born Jack, and approximately what time of day, if you know," she said.

"Like doing my star signs horoscope in the newspaper?" he replied lightly.

"No, Jack. He's going to use the Chinese feng shui methodology. It's an ancient system aligned to nature and the elements. Most Chinese believe in feng shui. Some won't start their day until they've checked on what their signs indicate for them for the next twenty-four hours. Lots of Chinese businesses have feng shui features around their offices and workplaces. Many non-Chinese who live here may not believe in it, but if they think their employees and workers do, they certainly don't publicly rail against it," explained May-Ling. "Anyway, this is just a bit of fun. What's your birth details?"

"Far be from me to push your feng shui away, Miss Wong. End of March, nineteen fifty-six, about four o'clock in the morning if I remember from my mother." She repeated the date and timing to the old man who began to leaf through one of the jotters on the table. For a few moments, he addressed himself once more in the local dialect to May-Ling.

"He says your birth-date is in the Year of the Fire Monkey," she explained. "You're strong-willed and make long-lasting friendships. You're also a hunter and a survivor. Money isn't an attraction in itself to you. You're not a financial gambler, but you take chances in other aspects of your life."

"Covers about one twelfth of the population of the planet, right?" Jack teased.

The fortune-teller showed no reaction. He made a slight humming sound as he found his way to the page he was looking for. He looked Jack straight in the eye and asked him in English to bring his face a little closer. Jack leaned forward. The old Chinaman stretched a hand toward Jack's face and trailed his thin fingers lightly twice across the Scotsman's forehead. With both hands he pressed with all his fingertips at the sides of Jack's head for about fifteen seconds.

Everything was quiet. Not even the noise from the street penetrated the room. The fortune-teller closed his eyes. When he opened them, Jack felt as if the stare went right through his own eyes. The husky voice broke the silence.

"Mister Jack," he addressed him, with a slow, sideway movement of his head, still peering intently, struggling to ensure a pinpoint focus.

He spoke softly. "You are accustomed to seeing people from the long sleep. Pain comes that you cannot keep away. The pain is needed to clear your heart of another soreness of a loss from a time more long ago."

Jack suddenly felt a familiar chill at the back of his neck.

The old man spoke again. "There are many things that may not be understood Mister Jack. But there is one thing I think you should understand."

Jack found his own voice, and asked, this time with respect, "What would that be, sir?"

"You should understand this. Your father was you. You are your father. Your father is you. This sleep pain will no longer come to you."

Jack had a lump at his throat. He did not reply to the fortune-teller, any flippancy he had brought into this chamber completely gone.

"Give me your left hand, please," the old man continued, extending a bony hand of his own across the table toward Jack.

Jack did as asked and placed his hand in the old man's. The fingers grasped Jack's gently. They were firm without clutching. The fortune-teller turned his eyes to the palm in front of him. Jack clearly heard an unmistakable small, sharp intake of breath. So did May-Ling and Malky.

"What is it, old man?" Jack asked, his instincts at full alert.

The man continued to stare at Jack's palm. After a long time he peered toward Jack's face. Where before there had been a passive look, a more serious, questioning shadow now flirted.

His voice sounded even quieter than before. "Why is it, Mister Jack, you are the only one who hears?"

"Hears what?" Jack asked, mystified.

"The music, Mister Jack." He paused. "The music of death. Why are you the only one who hears?"

A shiver went through Jack's body. On the surface he didn't understand what this man was talking about, but somehow, deep down inside him, he did.

How could that be? How could something he didn't understand, make sense?

* * * * *

They drove back to the Shangri La Hotel and Malky tried to make light of what had just happened with the fortune-teller. Jack responded in the same way, as if it was all truly a bit of melodramatic fun, but Malky knew his buddy thought otherwise and quickly moved the conversation on to other things. May-Ling said nothing.

The Irishman left them in the foyer and went off to check something in the business centre. Jack and May-Ling made their way to Jack's room without speaking.

Jack's mind struggled with the night's events. He admitted to himself the evening had been an unusual jumble of emotions. Normally a stranger to feelings of intensity, tonight May-Ling's gift of the jade stone had touched him. And the comfort of being in Malky's company. Finally, the strange gamut of exchanges in the fortune-teller's room jumped around in his head.

May-Ling spoke first as they sat together on the couch. "Jack, I'm sorry if the old man upset you."

"Oh, it's okay, just a little bit strange," he lied.

She squeezed his hand gently. "Let me share something with you, something I think's important for you to hear."

She took a deep breath and exhaled slowly. "I've heard you a couple of times talking in your sleep. And I can tell you, I've been there also. After Ben died. The mind sometimes won't let go of things, especially if like me, somehow you blame yourself for the death. Logically, we know it's stupid, but minds don't always work logically, particularly the unconscious mind. I got some useful help from a doctor friend for a few weeks when the nightmares became too bad. I don't think you need treatment, but understand it will pass. By the way, you're not responsible for your father's death either. What you've been fighting all these years is the anger that goes with it. Your dad leaving without giving you a chance to say a proper goodbye. Sometimes talking about it makes the whole thing easier to handle."

Jack Calder had never shared with anyone his feelings about his father's death. He started to try to tell May-Ling it didn't matter. Instead he began to talk about his father. About his family and the poverty haunting them growing up in the slums of Govan. About fighting against the child warriors in the Sudan. About the guerrillas in Serbia. May-Ling listened. And listened. And listened.

Neither had any awareness of how many hours passed before they crawled into bed. Where before, Jack had led their lovemaking in a robust way bordering on over-physical, this time May-Ling took control.

She placed a finger on his lips. No talk. When he pressed toward her, she pushed him back with a motion making it clear he wasn't to move. She would be in command. At her pace. In her way.

Geez, this is unreal, he thought. Here in bed, making love like this with May-Ling, seems the most natural thing in the world. He knew he had become fond of her, even after only a few short weeks. But was this being in love? He really didn't know. And what was all that about his father and the fortune-teller? Entangled in May-Ling's arms, he drifted into a deep, dreamless sleep.

CHAPTER 28

Dick de Jong sent May-Ling the names of the Fortune companies appearing on the remittance notices for Nils Bergman's account at Banque Wilhelm & Roche. She passed these on to the office administrator and told him to check them out.

In Tsuen Wan, the day dragged. They'd done all the checking and cross-checking and advised Hubert Meiss and Deryk Ostman the delivery would take place, as planned, in the early hours of Friday. Ostman's overnight flight into Hong Kong scheduled his arrival later the same morning. Jack wanted the goods to be at the Coliseum by the time the owner arrived.

Jules called from London and spoke to each of them, trying not to appear to be checking the details.

The day eased into afternoon, and drifted through into evening. A few minutes after ten o'clock, Donnie and Archie arrived with their squad.

Jack went over the ritual last-minute checks.

Back-up van to travel fifty yards behind the first team carrying the gems. Enough space for reaction if attacked. All members of both teams kitted in the Kevlar vests. Everyone wearing black with silver armbands, identifiable as friendlies. Weapons checked one last time. Boxes already loaded in the front vehicle. As they boarded, Jack and May-Ling paused and looked at each other, no words needed. Malky and Jack exchanged a knuckle punch. Ready to go.

At two o'clock, the guards opened the security gates. They were on their way to the Hong Kong Coliseum.

* * * * *

The roads carried light traffic, even at that time in the morning. Hong Kong never stops moving, day or night. They met a few vehicles, mostly taxis, on the agreed route taking them along the edge of the Kowloon Harbour. Then, instead of turning up through the inner ring as planted with the street whisperers, the vans continued via the exterior road by the sea.

Now there were no other vehicles in view. They approached the traffic lights at the intersection near the halfway point in the journey, slowing down for a red stop-light. Then the attack started.

The long, articulated lorry came screeching out from the side street and slammed its brakes hard, cutting off the way forward. Donnie and Archie in the covering van spotted it at the same time as the unit in the first vehicle. They braked to a halt thirty yards back from Jack and his partners. At once, two smaller trucks sped across the road behind the second team, locking in both security vehicles in the middle section of the highway.

Groups of armed men appeared from the blockers, front and rear, about half a dozen each, Jack guessed. They held AK47s and Uzi subs. This time, however, there were no masks. Jack and Malky read that instantly to mean this mob didn't intend to leave any witnesses. These guys owned this turf.

Kicking the side doors open, Jack shouted, "Go! Go! Go! Take 'em down time!"

He spun out first, MP5 blazing, followed by Malky, then May-Ling.

Roll and fire! Roll and fire! Keep low, aim upwards!

Malky rolled several times, away from Jack and May-Ling, firing as he went, creating an angle of crossfire. May-Ling, as planned, rolled towards the front wheel of the van, firing. Jack, plumb centre, rolled left and fired, rolled back right and fired, rolled back left again, firing.

Donnie and his men, disciplined from the second van, covered the team in front, already out of the vehicle shooting in spray bursts left and right behind at the attackers from the two trucks at the rear.

"Fire at will. Shoot to kill," ordered Donnie as his lads went into action.

Ahead, Jack watched as the assailants crumpled under the firepower from his own team. The same thing repeated behind him. To his right, one man raised a rocket-propelled grenade launcher towards the front van.

My God, they're prepared alright! That'll blow the van apart, and the driver inside with it!

His reaction was automatic. He rolled once more to the right and squeezed a burst toward the gunman. His target jerked backward and slid down the wheel of the truck. The grenade launcher spun away under the articulated vehicle.

Just as suddenly as the assault had begun, the shooting ceased. No incoming firepower remained. Front and back teams had done their jobs. The cordite stung the nostrils. Bodies scattered across the road beside the lorry, replicated at the rear of the second security van. The attackers hadn't expected this kind of repulse action. The element of surprise had been complete.

Donnie Mullen appeared beside Jack. He put his hand on his shoulder.

"Helluva take out, Jack. Couldn't have been sweeter," he said. He looked over to May-Ling. She was okay.

"Your boys alright?" asked Jack.

"Hundred percent," came the reply. "Where's Malky?"

Malky.

Jack turned to his left once more toward where Malky had rolled. His heart skipped a beat. The Irishman was lying on his side, twenty feet away, not moving.

Malky! Christ! Malky had been hit.

Jack reached him in an instant, with Donnie close behind. Blood seeped from Malky's left foot. He'd taken a bullet in the ankle. Across his chest, the scorch burns on the Kevlar vest traced the track of three or four more bullets. They hadn't penetrated the protective armour, but the sheer force would have been enough to smash Malky's ribs. He was still breathing, but unconscious.

Jack swallowed. Thank God!

"We need a medic now!" he heard himself shout.

"Relax, they're here already," said Donnie, as two men with medical bags appeared at Malky's side. "I had an unmarked ambulance trailing us, Jack. Just in case. Step back. Let these guys do their job." Jack noted how cool and in command the big Scottish cop remained. Another good man to have around in a fight. The rest of Donnie's men checked the results of their repulse onslaught.

Archie Campbell called across to his boss, "Chief, one of these cretins is still alive. He's in a pretty bad way. We'll need to get him to hospital too, right away, or he won't survive. The others are dead, nine in total."

Donnie gave his orders. "I couldn't care less if he makes it or not, but he might be useful as a squealer to nail the Half Moon Twins. Get the medics on him and post a security with him at the hospital. A guard for Malky too. Secluded rooms for both of them. Have the clean-up party take the rest of this scum away."

One of the paramedics tending Malky came over to where Jack and May-Ling stood with Donnie. "We've got a field-dressing on his ankle, and stemmed most of the blood flow, Chief. I reckon his ribs have taken a hammering."

"Why's he unconscious?" asked Donnie.

"He's concussed. I think he smacked his head on the kerbstone as he took the bullets," the medic replied. "There's a large contusion on his temple. Plus the impact of the hits, even with the vest, would cause his body to go into shock. One bullet got through and lodged in his left shoulder causing a lot of bleeding. We've put a field-dressing on that too. We'll get him into intensive care, but it's gonna be touch and go."

"Thanks," the three of them responded in unison.

Despite the early hour, traffic had built up on either side of the sealed area. A few more police squad cars redirected vehicles, turning them away from the crime scene.

The ambulance carrying Malky drove off. Donnie spoke to Jack. "So, do we carry on and deliver your goods now?"

"Yes. But we'll have to go back to the warehouse to get them," he replied.

"What?" The big policeman stared at Jack.

"You didn't think I'd be crazy enough to risk twelve million dollars on a decoy run did you? That stuff's still locked in the ISP vault. We can ferry it safely to the Coliseum now, right?"

"You mean all these guys would've picked were our ugly carcasses! Well I'll be damned," exclaimed Donnie, with a grin, "It never occurred to me they might not be aboard on this run. Good move, Jack. Let's go shift them now."

The convoy retraced its route to Tsuen Wan and loaded the gems. Two hours later, Gemtec's jewellery lay under multiple armed guard at the enlarged security vaults in the Hong Kong Coliseum.

Deryk Ostman would be briefed in the morning when he landed from Amsterdam.

CHAPTER 29

It was five o'clock in the morning. Adjoining rooms at the end of the corridor of the Intensive Care Unit bristled with heavily-armed plain-clothes detectives from Mullen's squad. May-Ling, Jack and Donnie Mullen came from the second delivery run to the Queen Elizabeth Hospital in Kowloon Park. The medical care available in Hong Kong equals any of the leading hospitals in Asia or Europe.

Malky McGuire flitted in and out of consciousness under heavy sedation. A couple of nurses and a senior doctor were in the room when his partners arrived to check up on his condition.

"What's the damage, Doctor?" asked Jack. "How badly hurt is he?"

"Five smashed ribs and extensive, severe bruising around the rib cage," responded the doctor, reading from a scribbled chart. "One bullet, as suspected, in his left upper shoulder has caused a fair mess. We've got the bleeding under control, which is a bonus. The ankle will need some reparatory surgery, but we'll wait a day or two to let the contusions subside before we decide when to operate. He took a helluva bang on the head as he fell. The bruising is extensive, and likely to take a while to disappear."

"No bullet penetration except for the shoulder and the ankle?" continued Jack.

"None, but the blows to his body from the force of the other bullets caused severe damage. He's a lucky man. They may well have been fatal for anyone not in such tough, physical condition. We'll keep him in the ICU for at least a week before we move him into a private ward."

"How long will he have to stay in?" asked May-Ling.

"Full recovery depends on his own body's response mechanisms. If he survives this first couple of days, the earliest expectation for getting him back to normal activity is around six to eight weeks."

"Thanks, doctor," said Jack. "Can we talk to him now?"

"I'd rather later. He's marginally conscious, but heavily medicated. He won't be aware of you at the moment. We'll let him know when he's properly able to take it in you were here to check up on him. His body's taken a hell of a pounding. He needs some breathing space right now. Can you come back later tonight?"

"Of course, doc, you're the boss," replied Jack.

They made their exit. Donnie crossed the hallway to the private room opposite to check out the injured attacker. Several wires connected the unconscious triad to a collection of machines. A Chinese detective in plain clothes guarded the patient, Jack noted. Donnie Mullen wanted to miss nothing in the event the man talked.

* * * * *

Nobody had slept for twenty-four hours but none of them were tired. The adrenaline had eased down after the attack. They sat in Donnie's office and watched from the fourth-floor window of the police headquarters the first swathe of dawn light break across the Hong Kong harbour. The volume of bustling traffic noise this early surprised Jack.

"What've we got from this morning's action?" the DCI asked.

"Our street whisperers were effective," Archie Campbell replied. "The reception party had the time, the place and the vehicles to hit."

"Archie, I agree with most of that," said Jack. "Your narks put the message out alright. They got the timing right. It was a no-brainer it would be ISP vehicles. But we didn't tell them where. We leaked word of the inner Kowloon Road, not the harbour ring. That came from another source."

Donnie Mullen nodded agreement. "Jack's spot on, Archie. The only people privy to the correct route include we four sitting here, Malky, and two other guys, Deryk Ostman and Hubert Meiss. Ostman's on a plane to Hong Kong as we speak."

"Which leaves Hubert Meiss," said May-Ling. "We purposely restricted the list of people in the loop. Nils

Bergman's involvement in the other hits, suggested Meiss is also tagged in somehow."

"Sorry, lads. I missed that one," said Archie.

"So far, of course, we only have the suspicion he might be involved," interrupted Donnie. "We've nothing concrete on him as yet. It's midnight in Holland, but I'll call Jens Kluvin in a few hours when he's awake and ask him to bring Meiss in for questioning. Let's lean on him and see what happens."

"Fine. Now, a bit of blanket time's called for," exhaled Jack. "Ostman'll be here later today. We'll need to catch up with him and give him the lowdown on this stuff."

"Jack, if you wouldn't mind, let me have a quiet word with Mr Ostman first when he arrives. This is an official investigation, and I'd like to follow some of the protocols."

"Sure." replied Jack. "Do you think he's implicated in hitting his own shipment?"

"Don't be racing off into unsubstantiated conclusions, Mr Calder," the big man chided. "As we've surmised, he's the only person outside of our group and Meiss privy to the delivery information."

"Could he be involved in taking down his own company's stuff?" repeated Jack.

"You're jumping to conclusions."

"You want to check him out anyway, right?"

"Sometimes it's better to let the cops do their police thing before any other stories get to the main players, Jack," said Donnie. "Helps us eliminate possible suspects, not tag them with stuff. We've a way of pitching questions that may lead Mr Ostman to show us whether he's involved or not without him knowing. Follow?"

"Yes, I guess so," smiled the ISP man. "I'm still learning."

CHAPTER 30

A few hours sleep and a hot shower later, Jack and May-Ling arrived back in Tsuen Wan. A telephone call to the hospital elicited the standard issue official report on Malky, still not conscious. The duty nurse confirmed the patient was as comfortable as could be expected given his injuries. Sedation would be reduced gradually over the next twenty-four hours.

The administration manager came by and dropped a sheet of paper on May-Ling's desk. "From the search at the Companies Registry."

"Thanks." May-Ling picked up the document and scanned the report.

"As we expected, Jack," she said, with a pleased look on her face. "All of the Fortune company names on Bergman's payment sources are companies linked to the Fortune Holding Group here in Hong Kong, as strong a tie-in as you're ever going to get."

"Good lady." he replied. "I'll call Donnie. It should be enough to justify a warrant to search the Fortune offices and it'll help Jens Kluvin too. He's itching for an excuse to hit their subsidiaries in Holland. This is the opener."

* * * * *

The confirmation from the ISP guys pleased DCI Mullen. He now had enough to get moving on the Fortune Group. He rang Jens as the Dutchman readied to leave for his office.

"We had an attempted hit on ISP's delivery for Gemtec early this morning on the way to the Trade Show building. Pretty heavy stuff," Donnie told him. "One serious casualty on our side. Malky McGuire took some bullets. He's got a few busted ribs and a smashed up ankle. The next couple of days are pivotal for him. We wasted nine of the bad guys, and we've one fighting to breathe in intensive care. We might get something out of him if survives."

"Excellent, Donnie, well done," replied the Dutchman. "Any tie-in to our triad friends yet?"

"The main reason for my call, my friend. The big news for you is all of the names on the list Dick sent over show a direct link to the Fortune Holdings Group. We're getting a warrant now to hit their offices here. I suggest you get yours primed too. Let's smack them at the same time, so no back-door exits for any of them, huh?"

"Sounds good," Jens agreed. "My lads've had the warrant ready for a few days. Just give me the signal when we're going in."

"One more thing, Jens," Donnie continued. "It's worth pulling in Hubert Meiss for a bit of heavy leaning. The finger's pointing to him being another Bergman."

"I must confess that comes as no real shock. Leave it to me. I'll get back to you later today. Have a good one. Goodbye."

* * * * *

Archie Campbell and his superior officer discussed the methodology for taking down the Fortune offices.

"Work with the Public Prosecutor yourself on this one, Archie," said Donnie. "The triad lads have ears inside some of the offices alongside his. He's as keen as we are to nail these bastards. Tell him this time we need to smack them hard and fast. With no-one else seeing documents across the lawyers' desks over there, we can guarantee no early leaks to our Half Moon friends. We want all-purpose search warrants covering all activities in Hong Kong and abroad. Bring him up to speed with Jens Kluvin's side of things also. That should get him excited."

Archie nodded. "Right, boss. We'll use our best bust and block teams when we drop the flag. They'll scream like hell."

"They won't be given time to react legally until at least the next day. "We'll move in around three in the afternoon just as Jens hits them early morning in Europe," said Donnie.

Archie got up. "I'll go over to the Prosecutor's office now. Catch you later."

Jack Calder talked on the phone for more than an hour with Jules, giving him the details of the night's activities. Jules fired off a barrage of questions and instructions, the main thrust being Malky's wellbeing.

"How is he? What time are you seeing him tonight? Make sure the hospital understands cost is no object. How's May-Ling? How are you? The delivery's well protected at the Coliseum? You're meeting with Ostman this afternoon? Assure him his goods are safe. Rotate the guards on irregular intervals at the Show. What else you got?" The list was comprehensive from the former commander.

Jack responded with a screed of information. "The lead from Holland on the payments to Bergman have tied in to Hong Kong for sure now. We're certain the bad guys are from the Half Moon Twins' triads, the Ching Tan Ka."

Jules replied, "And these are the people who tried to knock us over last night?"

"Yes, we're sure, boss."

"Next steps?"

"Donnie Mullen and Jens Kluvin are coordinating to hit their businesses on Monday," continued Jack. "They're arranging for bust and search warrants, the works."

"What about the Chan boys themselves?" asked Townsend. "Will they get taken in also?"

"A lot trickier, Jules. The twins move around here freely. Difficult to tie them in to any of the criminal stuff."

"Understood," said Jules. Jack figured his mentor's mind was working overtime.

"We've seen the type over the years, Jack, haven't we? I'm sure we can devise a way to nail them." Jack picked up on the change of tone in Jules' voice. His boss paused before speaking again.

"Why don't you reserve a room for me at the Shangri La? I'll come and join you guys for a while. I'll take a flight this evening and be with you tomorrow for lunch."

Jack Calder knew his former superior officer well. For Jules Townsend this had become personal.

Very personal.

* * * * *

In the early afternoon, Donnie Mullen dropped into Tsuen Wan unannounced.

"Got a call back from Jens half an hour ago," he told May-Ling and Jack. "They went to bring in Meiss. He's disappeared."

"What?" They both spoke as one.

"Gone. Done a Bergman. They had a couple of guys at his house. Nobody home. A neighbour says the car drove away in the morning. They checked the office. He hasn't turned up today."

"Did he ring them to say he wasn't going in?" asked May-Ling.

"No call," said Donnie. "His staff expected him as normal to discuss some of the revised shipping instructions for the gems in Hong Kong when the Trade Show's over."

"What's Kluvin's view?" asked Jack.

"Simple," replied the policeman. "Bergman's probably in South America by now. With Meiss on the way to join him. No trace at the airports for either of them. Jens believes Nils became spooked by a combination of May-Ling's enquiries, coupled with the risk of the local Fortune boys taking a hit on him. Discretion being the better part of valour, he did a runner."

"The same for Meiss?" he asked.

"No. He reckons Meiss is even smarter," explained Donnie. "Whatever the outcome of the attack on you guys in Hong Kong, whether successful or not, the line would trail back to Holland. With Bergman gone, he was the prime suspect. It adds up, Jack."

"Geez. I wish I could think as twisted as you cops do," joked Jack. "Would make this job a darn sight easier."

"I'm going over to the Peninsula Hotel now to meet with your Mr Ostman," Donnie told him. "Let's find out if my elimination theory works. See you later."

Jack and May-Ling looked at each other. Somehow the news of Hubert Meiss's disappearance blunted the satisfaction over the outcome of the previous twelve hours.

CHAPTER 31

DCI Mullen met first with Deryk Ostman at the Dutchman's suite at the Peninsula Hotel. The disappearance of his Head of Security shocked the jewellery chief as much as the attempted heist on the gems delivery.

Ostman had already been advised from Amsterdam Meiss hadn't turned up at the office in the morning. Chief Inspector Kluvin had left a message asking for a return call as soon as possible. He talked with Kluvin an hour before Donnie Mullen arrived in his hotel room. Even on long-distance telephone from Holland, he sensed Kluvin was unhappy with the turn of events. He could tell the Inspector nothing.

Now the Scotsman was scoping the same ground as his Dutch counterpart. He, however seemed a little more polite than his opposite number in Holland. Deryk Ostman realized each of their lines of questioning couched the attempt to discover if the gems boss had revealed to anyone else the real route plan for the journey to the Hong Kong Coliseum. He explained to the policeman he had not, leaving the arrow of suspicion pointing even more toward Hubert Meiss.

After Donnie left Ostman's suite, the Dutchman's next visitors were Jack Calder and May-Ling Wong. Beforehand, Donnie requested the security company officers not to discuss in detail the events of the previous night. Police matters would ultimately be the focus of legal action. Also, precise details of the attack were not public knowledge. The Anti-Triad Squad wanted to keep them private.

Discussion centred on the on-going security at the Trade Show. May-Ling covered the programme for the reverse shipments back to Amsterdam at the end of the week. A huge value at risk remained and ISP wanted to tie down the details.

The mystery of Hubert Meiss replicating the disappearance of Nils Bergman, made necessary yet again a review of internal processes at Gemtec in Amsterdam.

"Mr Ostman, may I propose Peter Dewer takes temporary control of the security arrangements in Holland until we complete another overhaul of Hubert's area?" asked Jack. "Dewer is a solid man, sir."

"Mr Calder," Ostman responded with dignity, "I could hardly entrust my business to ISP and then reject your recommendations. Given recent developments, my judgements in the past on these issues may prove to be somewhat flawed, although I understand no charges have been directed at anyone as yet."

"With respect, I disagree with you about your judgement, sir," said Jack. "You make judgements all the time on what you see in front of you. Nobody knowingly makes bad judgements. What you seem to have the good sense to do, which I may say not many do, is to make follow-up judgement calls to rectify matters. I'm sure we'll get all of this sorted out soon."

"I hope so, Mr Calder," said Ostman.

May-Ling noted the news of the injuries inflicted on Malky McGuire also shook the Dutchman. He asked to accompany them in the evening to visit their partner at the hospital. They agreed to travel together to check out the set-up at the Coliseum first and continue on to the ward afterward.

"Tell me, Mr Calder," he said, with obvious concern. "With this second attack on Gemtec in a month, do you believe this originates from inside my company?"

"Yes, Mr Ostman. We'd be lying to say otherwise," replied Jack. "The overwhelming suspicion pointed squarely to Bergman and now to Meiss. We're trying to gather solid evidence to back that up. However, with neither man available to talk with us, we'll keep hunting this stuff down. Chief Inspectors Kluvin and Mullen have a lot of resources focused on these cases. In the meantime, our primary concern is to protect and return your merchandize safely to Holland."

"Much appreciated, Mr Calder," said Ostman. "Now, shall we go and have a look at the show arrangements?"

* * * * *

The display stands and booths clustered elegantly over the broad sweep of the Coliseum's largest internal arena. Armed security attended every corner. Jack made a careful note of the number of general guards in the vast hall, as well as the numbers at the individual presenters' allotted spaces. He thought the balance tallied about right.

All of the key global players in the jewellery trade were represented. The business generated at this Show would determine for many the profitability of their companies not just for the current year, but also for several years to come.

Deryk Ostman spent a lot of time talking with the Gemtec local manager regarding their booth arrangement and display presentation. The guards were from ISP, of course. Jack and May-Ling walked him through the daily security procedures within the Coliseum. The gems and other hardware would be under lock and key each evening with an allotted space exclusively for Gemtec in the large vault at the rear of the hall. Overall security in the Trade Show dictated a set time each morning and evening for the movement of each exhibitor's goods. No overlaps. The procedures satisfied Ostman. He doesn't look like a man about to steal his own merchandize thought Jack.

* * * * *

The aching in Malky's chest and ribcage easod. He liked least the drip-feed tubes inserted in each arm. A tube at his nostrils fed extra oxygen to his lungs. Other instruments attached to machines at the side of his bed cluttered his upper body. He hadn't been given any food since his arrival, and hadn't wanted to eat anyway. It took a while for him to realize the tubes supplied his sustenance for the meantime.

The doctor spoke to him in the afternoon, when some of the swirling fog had cleared from Malky's brain.

"Mr McGuire, you've taken five separate hits from the bullets of a sub-machine gun, one of which lodged in your shoulder. Without the armoured vest you would be dead. Thankfully, your own physical condition is excellent. Several ribs are fractured with attendant, severe bruising. Fortunately, none of these is life-threatening."

The Irishman grunted.

"Your ankle took another bullet, probably a ricochet. This will need a minor operation to restructure your foot. We intend to sort that out tomorrow evening, under general anaesthetic. If the damage to your ribs had been worse, we wouldn't consider such an operation for at least another week, in which case the prospect of full recovery on your ankle would have been reduced. You're a remarkably strong man, Mr McGuire."

"Do you mean I can't go dancing this weekend, doc?" Malky mumbled, slurring his words from the medication, but damned if he couldn't get a laugh going.

"Maybe next weekend, Mr McGuire," chuckled the doctor. "Maybe next weekend."

The permission granted to May-Ling, Jack and Deryk Ostman to enter his room followed a warning from the Chinese staff nurse to take no more than twenty minutes, as Mr McGuire was "a very sick man."

"Aye, we've known that for years," joked Jack, on the way toward his buddy's bedside. He felt enormous relief, that although still in intensive care, his pal had moved out of immediate danger.

They circled Malky's bed and the Irishman's eyes followed each of them. He looked tired.

"Hi guys," he said.

The nurse broke in across them. "You'll be quiet now, Mr McGuire, if you please. Doctor says you're on listening brief only for today. That way we'll get you well quicker."

"Okay, sweetheart," he replied.

"Jules is flying in, Malky," said Jack. "He'll visit you the day after tomorrow. The doc told us you're getting a new, supersonic foot fixed. Be no holding you back now, you daft Irish Mick. By the way, the guy with the Uzi asked for his bullets back."

A broad smile broke across Malky's face, the dark, gallows humour a mark of the SAS.

May-Ling noticed first. The piece of jade she had given him at the market lay on the side table by the bed. Malky had carried it with him on the delivery run.

He caught her eyeing the stone. "I told ye we Irish are as superstitious as the rest of ye, didn't I?" he struggled to say with another huge smile.

Ostman greeted him stiffly and wished him a speedy recovery. A large bouquet of flowers in the room with a Gemtec card attached adorned the ward table. The staff nurse shepherded them out after twenty minutes. By then, Malky's eyes began to close. Sleep is a deep healer.

CHAPTER 32

Donnie Mullen and Archie Campbell joined May-Ling and Jack after Ostman returned to his own hotel.

"The search warrants for the Chans' companies are ready and primed to go," said Donnie. "I've spoken to Jens. We'll smack them together on Monday during office hours. He goes in at nine in the morning local time in Rotterdam and Amsterdam. We take them here at three in the afternoon. We've arrest warrants for Kai and Choi in Holland. By the time they draw breath to alert their lawyers, we'll have our hands on a load of documents, and before they get their counter-warrants from the courts, we'll lose a few of the files. We're going in with at least a dozen guys in each location." He looked around the group. "That should cause a little bit of a stir for Jonnie and Jimmie Half Moon," he finished with satisfaction.

"Terrific, Donnie," replied May-Ling. "Any news yet from Jens on Meiss?"

"Nothing so far. Same as Bergman. Oh, he surfaced a couple of names as payees on the funds sent to the bank in Bolivia. Philip Jacoob and John Vogel. Donnie raised his eyebrows. "Mean anything to you guys?"

Jack and May-Ling shook their heads. "Maybe Jules has some ideas. We'll talk to him when he gets here tomorrow," said Jack.

"How about the triad in the intensive care unit?" asked May-Ling. "Any luck?"

"No. He's conscious now, but only just. The gang didn't expect much in the way of resistance. None of them were wearing protective vests. He took a bullet in the shoulder. Probably be a couple of days yet before we get anything from him. Tattoos on the other bodies indicate the Ching Tan Ka. We made identities on two of them. We've Chinese officers contacting their families to see if our offer of help to them can elicit anything else useful to us. You know how that works, May-Ling."

She nodded.

"One other piece." said Archie. "The articulated lorry belongs to the Fortune Group. It won't tie them in legally to anything, as they'll claim it was stolen, but it bolsters our circumstantial case. The guns are untraceable, as you'd expect," he continued. "We keep doing the good things cops do. I'm sure we're getting closer to them. Tomorrow afternoon after the raids, they'll be rattled as hell."

"Which means there may be some retaliatory action," said Donnie. "Jack, I'd advise you to be even more vigilant at the warehouse. May-Ling, you're a name to these guys. Keep your wits about you."

"Understood completely," replied Jack. "I already switched to triple guards on the premises. We'll keep May-Ling close also."

She smiled at him. He could count on that.

* * * * *

The Cathay Pacific flight to Hong Kong was comfortable enough. Jules Townsend was seated in the forward business class, which allowed his six-foot frame to avoid the cramping experienced on some other airlines. He always slept well on long flights, avoiding the freely available alcohol in preference for plenty of soda water.

Jack met him at Kai-Tak airport. "How was your flight," he asked as Jules emerged into the receiving area.

"Asleep for most of it," came the reply. "Is Malky able to take visitors?"

"His ankle's supposed to be getting operated on this evening, but we could go now, said Jack. "They won't have started the pre-op yet, I'm sure. You don't want to wait until tomorrow?"

"No time like the present," Jules insisted.

Jack nodded. Some things never changed, Jules looking after his team first and foremost.

* * * * *

The Chinese staff nurse bustled around her charge like a possessive mother goose.

Malky was more alert, waiting to go in for his operation. He broke into a grin when Jules and Jack loomed large through the ward doorway.

"Thought ye said ye weren't comin' in until tomorrow, after me face-lift surgery," he jested.

"You know what this guy's like," replied Jack, pointing to their boss. "Wanted to check how much you're swinging the lead."

"How you feeling, Malky?" asked Jules, scrutinizing the various tubes still attached to parts of the Irishman's body.

"Apart from havin' an elephant sittin' on my chest, and a bad tackle on the ankle the referee never even blew for, never been better," Malky replied. "Should be sprintin' out o' here by the weekend."

Jack rolled his eyes to the ceiling with a mock 'tut-tut'.

"Common sense was never your strong suit, Malky," teased Jules. "Just as well they've hidden your trousers somewhere."

The nurses arrived for Malky's pre-operation procedure and Mother Goose ushered them out in a way even former commandos couldn't resist.

Jules wasn't done yet, however.

They went looking for the senior doctor in charge of

Malky, tracking him down to a small office at the other end of the ward corridor.

"Good day, Doctor," said Jules politely. "I'm Julian Townsend. I understand you're looking after my guy, McGuire."

"Hello." The doctor gestured for his unexpected guests to take a seat. "Your guy, McGuire, as you call him, is a lucky man, Mr Townsend. He's come within an inch of being killed. I'm astonished at the body strength he must possess to have ridden the bullets. I'd say he's used up a fair number of his nine cat-lives this week."

"You're right, doctor," replied Jules. "I can't express to you how grateful I am for the care he's getting. He'll insist on leaving the hospital at the earliest possible moment. He'd jump on a bus now if you'd let him. I'd be ultra-grateful to you if you ensure he's kept in here for a week or two beyond the time he tells you he's ready to go. All his medical expenses of course are covered by my company."

The doctor replied with an understanding wink. "I read you clearly Mr Townsend. Mr McGuire will only do himself more damage unless he follows my advice to the letter. You have my word he won't be leaving here for at least a month."

"Thank you, doctor. We'll be dropping by regularly for the next few days. I look forward to your updates. Goodbye."

* * * * *

For most of the way to the Shangri La Hotel, Jules was deep in thought. Jack knew better than to try to talk across the silence. His boss treated the team as if they were his own brothers. Nothing much ever seemed to ruffle the Major on the surface, but for attacking his people and assaulting Malky, someone somewhere was going to be made to pay.

CHAPTER 33

The conversation on the secure line was terse. Jimmie Chan was not accustomed to failure anywhere within his organization. However, he was too old in the tooth for a knee-jerk reaction. His instructions to his brother were brief and to the point.

"We behave as normal, Jonnie. Life carries on as usual. We take our time and make sure this nuisance goes away permanently. You'll need some planning, not full frontal brute force, do you understand?"

"Of course. The broader business is more important than the little setback from last night. I'll take care of the new mosquitoes."

Jonnie's voice remained calm, but he seethed inside. Enforcement fell to him and his team had screwed up. Big time. Someone had to pay.

He stepped into the warehouse where his men waited with the two lieutenants who had been in charge of the thwarted attacks. The beatings with wooden clubs had smashed their features into unrecognizable bloody pulp. Half a dozen gang heavies surrounded the hapless pair, tied to a couple of bamboo-backed chairs in the godown.

"Do it," Jonnie commanded. Behind each seated casualty an executioner waited. On the signal from the boss, they stepped forward and looped piano-wire garrottes around the lieutenants' throats. They died conjoined in their failure.

Another message to the street.

* * * * *

The Peninsula Hotel's reputation for comfort and elegance permeated Deryk Ostman's suite. An extensive sitting room held an assortment of fine-quality furnishings, including a five-piece set of Italian lounge chairs and settees. Chinese prints along each wall area reflected the Hong Kong ownership of the hotel. A walnut-wood panelled, in-room bar provided a generous range of spirit bottles. A large refrigerator disguised as a piece of furniture matching the bar occupied an entire corner.

The Dutchman had agreed to meet with the ISP team in the early evening. Jules and Ostman greeted each other with mutual respect.

"Mr Townsend, I'm grateful for your involvement with Gemtec these past few weeks," said Ostman. "This criminal activity is quite extraordinary. With Hubert Meiss's disappearance I'm more bewildered than ever. I understand in our business there's always a serious security risk, however, the scale of these attacks is beyond my comprehension. I'd be grateful for your thoughts now."

Jules sipped his coffee before answering. "Mr Ostman, you're not expected to be in the business of coping with criminals. That's our job, and the job of the police. Our assessments of your company's security arrangements stack up well as far as standard operating procedures and processes are concerned. No amount of excellent organization can defend you against internal sabotage. Especially coming from senior officers within your own ranks. Jack Calder already gave you our view that Bergman and Meiss are directly implicated in all of these attacks to date. We're working with the authorities in Holland and here in Hong Kong to try to track down the criminals.

"Am I correct in thinking the local Chinese triad people are involved?" Ostman asked.

"Yes. We're certain," replied Jules. "We've narrowed down the involvement to one particular gang, called the Ching Tan Ka. These men attacked the latest delivery here in Kowloon. We think it likely they were also the assailants in Utrecht."

"So, how do we deal with this?" asked the Gemtec owner.

"First of all, in the short term, we continue with the strict enforcement of the security protocols already in place," Jules responded. "We may strengthen the armed headcount here and there, but ISP's present coverage is more than adequate to keep your business intact."

"And longer term?" queried Ostman.

"Longer term we have some ideas to remove much of the threat for the future," said Jules.

"Would you care to share them with me?"

"Mr Ostman, I'm sure your father would've taught you sometimes it's better to restrict information when dealing with security issues."

Jack glanced at Jules. Jules knew about Ostman's father?

Ostman nodded. "I understand Mr Townsend. Let me just say, whatever means you use to bring the criminals in this series of events to account, will meet with my accord."

Clear enough, mused Jack. Good man.

"I thought it might, Mr Ostman. Thanks for your support," said Jules, placing his coffee cup on the table. "Now, I think we have to get back. We've a bit of planning to do this evening. We'll be in touch again tomorrow. Goodnight."

* * * * *

"What do you know about Ostman's father?" Jack asked Jules, when they had reconvened in Jules' room at the Shangri La.

"His dad was a leading member of the Dutch underground during the Nazi occupation," replied Jules. "He ran his men from a secret warehouse on the outskirts of Amsterdam, about two hundred of them. By the time the war finished, only a few dozen remained. Many of them died in direct fighting with the Nazis. Others were captured and suffered horrific torture before being executed." May-Ling frowned at the thought of the executions of these brave partisans.

Jack shook his head. "How did you learn all this, Jules?"

"The SAS intelligence files back in Hereford, Jack. Remember, I still possess a fair amount of clout. Before engaging with Deryk Ostman, I had one of my old contacts check him out, as well as the family business history. It always pays to do your homework on who you're dealing with."

"Right," said Jack. "Which reminds me, Jens Kluvin gave us a couple of names appearing as payees for the funds sent to Bolivia from Bergman's account in Holland. One guy called Philip Jacoob, and the other, John Vogel. Can you get your man to check these out for us too?"

"Jacoob and Vogel, huh?" Jules responded. "Okay, will be done."

"While he's at it, it'd be useful to have him trawl Nils and Hubert's names at the same time. See if these lads have any track in Chile or Bolivia?"

"Not a bad idea, too," said his boss. "You're getting smart in your old age, Jack. Maybe something's rubbing off from Donnie Mullen."

Jules spoke to May-Ling. "Now Miss Wong, I need you to unload intelligence on Jonnie and Jimmie Half Moon, as full a profiling as you can give me."

"I can get Donnie Mullen's input," she responded. "He'd be glad to help. He knows these guys inside out."

Jules shook his head. "No. This time we leave DCI Mullen and his squad out of this. Let's create a little professional distance between us for the moment. You'll understand why in a while."

* * * * *

An hour later, May-Ling had brought Jules up to speed on the Chan twins and their operations. The input from Donnie's conversation with them over dinner the previous week held particular interest for the former Major.

Jules went over and over the information, paying his usual attention to detail.

"The biggest competition from the other triad gangs is whom?" he asked, for the third time.

"The Mok Kwong Cho," she replied yet again, knowing Jules needed to get the full intelligence embedded in his mind.

"Wednesday evenings, both Chans are out playing? Jonnie with his lady love at the Heavenly Clouds motel, and his brother doing his mahjong thing, right?"

"Right."

Jules got up and started to pace the room. His officers watched him without interruption. The action program was forming, He'd share it with them soon enough.

He stopped and asked May-Ling, "When Jonnie goes to Wong Tai Sing with his girlfriend, does he take security with him?"

"Of course. Neither of the Half Moons ever moves without armed bodyguards, a minimum of two with each of them," she responded. "If Jonnie is on his own with the lady, you'd expect a couple of heavies alongside. At Jimmie's mahjong session the other players also have armed company, about half a dozen at the villa in Sai Kung."

"Outside or inside?"

"Only two or three outside. The rest would be inside serving the drinks and chow, just hanging around."

"I presume these boys are not protection to rebuff the likes of Donnie Mullen, but for the friendly neighbourhood competition, such as the Mok Kwong Cho?"

"Correct," said May-Ling.

Jules paced the room once more. Several minutes later he sat down abruptly. Jack and May-Ling prepared to listen, as Jules began.

"Here's how it should work…"

* * * * *

Another hour passed while Jules laid out his thoughts. Jack asked a few questions which Jules answered, finally bringing a smile from May-Ling.

"Yes, I think that should work very well," she said.

CHAPTER 34

Most of Holland awoke to an early summer Monday morning of low-lying rain clouds. No pedestrians lingered on the walkways on their way to work.

Jens Kluvin conducted the pre-dawn, last-minute briefing. Today's operation would be a key component in putting some bad guys away for a long time.

At nine o'clock in the morning, Detective Inspectors Bram Carbet in Rotterdam and Dick de Jong in Amsterdam moved in against the Dutch subsidiaries of the Fortune Holding Group. The detectives led teams of fifteen officers each on the raids on Alliance Trading Company Limited and Pan Asia Export Company Limited. As well as the Anti-Triad squad members, the teams had additional support seconded from other units of the Serious Crimes Squad. Carbet and de Jong held the search warrants. Jens Kluvin and Donnie Mullen determined to send the toughest possible message to the Chans, causing maximum uproar and disruption to their operations. The gloves were off. The squad commandeered filing cabinets and computers wholesale, swept papers lying on office desks into large cardboard boxes, even tipping litterbins in on top. They politely told staff the Dutch police had the company's business under investigation and they should leave the offices immediately. And, no, the officers had no idea when employees might be permitted to return.

The detectives arrested and handcuffed Messrs Choi and Kai with much publicity and noise. Pre-alerted press photographers captured the news for their respective publications, assuring headlines for the following morning's newspapers. Phone calls from Kluvin's office to the editorial chiefs with unattributable loaded statements provided ample copy for their readership.

At the same time, which meant three o'clock in the afternoon in Hong Kong, Archie Campbell led a larger team into the main headquarters of the Fortune Holdings Group. Chinese officers instructed startled staff to leave their desks and go home. The squad seized piles of documents along with every computer in sight. They did not arrest the general manager, merely inviting him to accompany the police to assist in their enquiries. The cameras of pressmen from the three main newspapers in Hong Kong captured the raid.

* * * * *

In Holland, the courts rebuffed the expected swift response from company lawyers wanting to post bail for the arrested executives. Jens Kluvin had telephoned his friendly counterparts in the judiciary to ensure no such consideration should be permitted to suspects in a series of armed robbery murders. This promised to be a difficult time for the Fortune legal teams.

The general manager in Hong Kong was held for questioning for more than twelve hours and released without charge at four in the morning, the message from the authorities well and truly delivered.

A flurry of lawyers' protests and claims against the raids followed in all three centres. The documents and computers taken from the Fortune offices remained securely in police possession. Donnie Mullen, like Jens Kluvin, had good friends in influential government departments, rendering the Chans' legal machine, for once, impotent. Pay-back time.

Accounting experts pored through the data with mountains of paperwork to be scrutinized, much of it ordinary commercial documentation found in any organization. The teams combed for links to the criminal side of the business, strong enough to stand up in a court of law.

The search ultimately turned up the various payment flows to subsidiaries around the world. This promised to keep rafts of lawyers occupied for several months to come.

Throughout the Tuesday, police watchers of the Half Moon Twins reported no unusual change in activity, no difference in their daily routines.

Smart and cool, admitted Donnie. The Chans gave no outward sign the events had anything to do with them.

Through the contacts May-Ling maintained with her former colleagues, Jules Townsend also learned the Chans weren't altering their behaviour patterns. This came as no surprise to him and suited the action plan that he, Jack and May-Ling discussed a couple of nights before.

* * * * *

With May-Ling driving, Jules and Jack undertook a focused tour of Wong Tai Sin and Sai Kung. Early morning visits to the Heavenly Clouds Motel were never likely to disturb any guests, short-term or otherwise. The Motel's business traffic generally started as darkness fell.

They began a meticulous reconnaissance of the place. The layout and entrance to the building were straightforward, the pale-green, exterior walls and shrubbery intended more for concealment than open planning. The single-storey structure contained twenty semi-detached rooms, and one stand-alone bungalow. The bungalow was reserved every Wednesday for the exclusive use of Jonnie Half Moon. It stood almost hidden in the rear of the premises. By its side, an open-fronted, covered carport gave further protection from weather and unwelcome eyes, the nearest structure ten yards in front and to the left, out of view.

The next port of call, twenty minutes drive away, brought their unmarked van to a parking area forty yards from Jimmie's mahjong villa in Sai Kung. The parking area, diagonally across the road from the building, served in daytime as a dropping off point for entry to a national park. Their late morning presence attracted no attention.

In the evening during darkness hours, no other casual vehicles would be expected.

Jack and Jules used binoculars to scan the property. No neighbouring buildings within five hundred yards encroached on either side. Unlike the motel in Wong Tai Sin, obstructive walls were unnecessary in Sai Kung.

The grounds landscaped down to the roadside for about thirty yards in the front garden, with ample bush and tree plantation visible. Paved driveways with parking facilities for up to three cars each bordered the sides of the building. At the rear of the structure, a line of high foliage blocked intruders. Countryside extended into the distance.

The entrance to the villa boasted a set of heavy, brown, main doors, one half already bolted open. Inlaid carvings of standing lions adorned the door panels as silent guardians to the entry point. What looked like a short anteroom led into a hallway. Slatted, wooden blinds shuttered the windows. Jack estimated six or seven good-sized rooms in the whole building.

They took much longer in the review of this site than the one in Wong Tai Sin.

Their reconnaissance complete, they stowed the binoculars and returned to Tsuen Wan to refine the action plan.

* * * * *

The ICU room at the hospital resembled a traffic jam. As Malky's ISP mates arrived, Deryk Ostman said his goodbyes to the Irishman. Despite the Trade Show being in full swing, the Dutchman took time daily to visit Malky.

The operation on Malky's foot was a success according to the senior surgeon in charge of the theatre, with, incredibly, only minor fractures to the bones. The main structure was sound. The surgeon estimated the recovery process at three weeks before any possible light physiotherapy. The pain in his ribs subsided, and the medication dosage reduced daily. Nature began to take its healing course, but he wasn't yet eating normal meals.

The news on the triad was in complete contrast. The casualty died of his injuries on the Monday morning, much to the chagrin of DCI Mullen. He lamented the lack of possible evidence they might have extracted from the man, and the chance of a direct link to the Chans.

Donnie Mullen and Archie Campbell also visited Malky's bedside every day. They found common ground to argue over in the national rugby capabilities of Scotland and Ireland. Jack guessed they came out all square despite the two to one debating advantage of the Scots duo.

Jules cast a quiet, professional eye over the standing guard Donnie had in place. No worries. Time to go chill out until tomorrow evening.

* * * * *

The ward night shift was a couple of hours old. Malky drifted in and out of sleep. Muscle aches kicked in as the medicine dosage reduced further. His ribs and ankle ached like shit. The staff nurse, Mother Goose, constantly filled a large jug of fortified juice on the bedside cabinet together with a half-pint tumbler. Still only liquids allowed at this stage. Presents of fruit and chocolates were hidden away from the Irishman.

Malky's duty guard looked up as the night orderly approached, pushing his trolley laden with magazines, bedpans, water bottles and other odds and sorts. Both men nodded a greeting. The orderly made to enter the room and the guard stood up to block the way. "Not to be disturbed, my friend," he said.

"Okay. No problem," came the reply in Cantonese. As the man made to turn the trolley around, his right hand moved swiftly. The guard didn't see the knife until it was too late. The blade entered just below his left ear, and in seconds he was lying dead in the empty corridor. The attacker peered inside. The patient was motionless. So far so good.

He dragged the corpse into the room, making it invisible from the corridor. Still no movement from the bed. Now to finish the job.

He clutched his weapon and crept toward the sleeping form. A piercing scream halted him dead in his tracks. Mother Goose rushed in from the corridor toward the assailant. In reaction to this unexpected interruption he turned in one motion and slashed at the woman. His strike hit the nurse across her arm and chest as he stabbed a second time. She slumped with a cry to the floor.

The woman's scream startled Malky awake. In his partly-medicated state he struggled to get out from the sheets. The attacker ran at him, but the thrust towards his intended victim's neck was countered by a vice-like grip which pulled the lunge downwards. He pushed forward again with the knife despite the hold on his wrist. The defected blow caused the blade to enter Malky's thigh.

The former commando was now in automatic survival mode. He felt the deep incision and determined the guy was not getting a second stab at him, but he was going to lose a ton of blood.

His right hand grasped the glass tumbler from the bedside cabinet. With a single fluent movement he broke the rim against the wood and rammed the jagged remnants into the throat of his attacker and twisted.

Malky's left grip held the man fast, making it impossible to retreat from the embrace. He thrust the glass further into the man's neck until he felt him drop lifeless to the floor. Pulling the knife from his leg, he tried to stem the blood with the bedsheet, but his head spun violently.

He was barely aware of the injured Mother Goose sobbing at his ear as she pressed the emergency panic button by the side of his bed.

Total darkness descended.

CHAPTER 35

Jules listened intently to the doctor's summation on Malky's condition. Donnie had joined him in the office where Jules had sought out the doctor the previous day.

"He lost a lot of blood, Mr Townsend," he said, tapping the medical notes on his desk. "We transfused more than six pints before we got him stabilised. The drugs are counteracting much of the flow issues now, but he'll be staying in intensive care for at least another couple of weeks. He's not out of the woods yet."

"And the nurse?"

"Two wounds, one no more than a flesh cut. The second caused some concern. She's also stable now. Thank God she stayed conscious long enough to press the emergency button, otherwise both of them would be dead."

"Thanks, doctor. I'm deeply grateful for all you've done for us," said Jules, rising to leave. "I don't want to interrupt your work any more than we have already. He and Donnie stepped out of the doctor's room into the corridor.

"Sorry about your man, Donnie. What've you got in mind now?"

"My man had no family, but he was a good officer, Jules," the policeman replied. "The bastard who knifed him had the usual signature tattoos. I've no doubts the Half Moon boys ordered this. There's no direct hard link yet. My hands are tied," said Donnie with a frustrated shrug of his massive shoulders. "Of course, we'll put a lot of heat on the street, but I'm damned if we'll be able to get near the Chans. My reports tell me they're still going about their business as if nothing unusual has hit them.

Jules grunted as he continued to listen. "As you can see, I've four armed specialists to look after Malky. Experience tells us they won't attack here again. I trust you've already heightened personal security at your own operations?"

The ISP chief nodded. "We did so after the attempt on May-Ling. We're a small group in Hong Kong. We've taken full precautions for all of our people. This'll be resolved soon, Donnie."

Mullen raised a questioning eyebrow towards the Englishman.

Jules stared back. "Time to get to work. We've got a Trade Fair to protect."

* * * * *

The developments of the past few days troubled Jimmie Chan. He couldn't recall in the last twenty years when their business had been under such direct threat.

Gang warfare was always easily dealt with through the use of money and men. That was food and drink to him. Jonnie had learned at first hand in the early years, his older brother's ruthlessness. Executions, the more violent the better, established their reputation. You messed with the Half Moon brothers at your mortal peril.

Over two decades, the Wednesday evening mahjong sessions at the Sai Kung villa had been an effective means of controlling his top lieutenants. There'd been a few changes in the members over the years, but basically the same core of close confidantes. They still discussed business, more at a strategic level than mundane day to day operational issues.

Jimmie and Jonnie were real twins, with Jimmie born minutes before his brother. Regardless of how marginal the time difference at birth, Jimmie truly was the senior partner.

He had primary control and direction over the sophisticated network of criminal businesses underpinning their enterprises. Strategy and alliances became his forte. On the other hand, Jonnie learned well, excelling in enforcement and execution of their plans. The brothers attended business school in the United States, and both developed proficiency in manipulating the legal and financial systems to complement their commercial activities.

Jimmie continually ran the structure through his head. Until now, an impregnable distance had existed between the criminal sources of income and the prima facie legitimate companies. Money laundering was down to a fine art, the best financial minds and legal talent high on the payroll.

All these men here tonight reflect that talent, he thought. All criminal by any definition. And untouchable. He allowed himself a smile. The next morning he'd get Jonnie switched into full-scale mosquito eradication.

This evening they'd play as usual.

Dinner always consisted of small finger-foods and plenty of brandy and scotch. Jimmie liked the players to rotate their positions at the two tables throughout the sessions until everyone had partnered everyone else at least once in the course of the night. Gambling was an integral part of the game. The objective wasn't to win large amounts of money. The same modest sum per player committed each Wednesday capped the amount any one man lost, small beer to the wealth sitting at the tables. Just having something at stake satisfied the Chinese basic instinct for gambling.

Bodyguards doubled as attendants, but weren't allowed into the gaming room unless summoned by the ringing of a bell at each table. Even small talk was confidential among these big hitters in this close-knit club.

Punctuality was a must for Jimmie Half Moon. The mahjong sessions always began at exactly nine o'clock. Finishing time varied into the early hours each Thursday morning.

This evening's session was destined to end more abruptly than usual.

CHAPTER 36

Detail, detail, detail.

An hour before leaving Tsuen Wan, Jules retraced the ground one more time. May-Ling and Jack listened for any nuance of discomfort. There was none.

Two unmarked vehicles with darkened windows were primed and ready to go. Fuel levels in the cars checked. All-black body kit, no silver identification strips needed this evening. Black-faced balaclava hoods. Stilettos. Lugers with silencers. AK47s triple-checked with ammunition. None of the usual MP5s on this occasion. At nine-thirty, the two vehicles emerged from the warehouse gates. May-Ling, alone, drove the front car, Jack driving the second with Jules as passenger.

Under instruction, May-Ling tempered her aggressive driving to avoid attracting attention. The double-car convoy made its way north through thick traffic toward Sai Kung, the first order of priority to check Jimmie Half Moon and his mahjong players were already in session.

"We take nothing for granted," Jules had cautioned earlier. "These guys have seen their main business offices busted this week. Up until now they've continued to act as if nothing unusual has happened. Let's hope they carry on as normal. We don't want the mahjong night cancelled, or it's back to the drawing board."

The traffic thinned out as the heavier-populated environs of Kowloon gave way to the countryside. By the time they reached Sai Kung, it had dwindled to a trickle of vehicles.

Jimmie Chan didn't use bright lighting around his villa. The watchers could still identify what they needed to confirm. An array of high-value cars stood parked in the driveways and roadside next to the building.

The ISP team drove by twice. Satisfied the evening game was well in progress, May-Ling stopped her car at the same morning lay-by parking area, forty yards away.

No other vehicles appeared at that time of night. She cut the engine and turned off the lights, her brief now to sit and observe until the return of Jack and Jules. It was important to note if anyone entered or left in their absence. Two bodyguards strolled outside the premises. They stood together, smoking and talking, taking no notice of the darkened car some way across the highway.

* * * * *

Tonight had been the most difficult yet for Debbie Devlin.

Jonnie tied her wrists and ankles spread-eagling her body on the bed. They regularly used the whip on each other, but an anger she hadn't known before drove the lashing he served up for this session.

Large welts raised on her breasts and buttocks. Blood started to leak from the bruises on her thighs. She tried to signal him to stop, but the handkerchief gagging her mouth caused only agonized moans.

After an eternity the beating stopped. His eyes grew wild and his breathing hurried in gasps. She could sense his body relax and then tighten as he approached her once more. He placed a large pillow under her buttocks and started to caress between her legs. Despite the pain from the cuts, she began to feel aroused. He entered her slowly, almost teasing her. His rhythm grew stronger and she started to orgasm, her moaning now sexually driven. Repeatedly he thrust into her, until with a shudder he exploded inside her.

He untied her and offered a small towel to dab at the blood. "Sorry, my dear Debbie. I didn't mean to be so rough. Now it's my turn. Tonight I need you to hurt me, you understand?"

"Sure, Jonnie. No problem." She knew he needed this, even if she couldn't really fathom why. But who was she to argue? He was paying.

He lay face downward as she repeated the cross position tie-ups on his wrists and ankles. She began to whip him across the lower back, moving gradually on to his backside.

"Harder, Debbie, harder," he whispered as he tried to raise his buttocks toward her blows. She hit him several times more with as much strength as she could muster with a growing sense of disbelief. Were they both mad?

He nodded, enough. She moved off the bed and walked toward the bathroom. He always remained tied up until she finished her shower, his way of coming down from the high.

* * * * *

The ISP men departed for Wong Tai Sin. The journey to the Heavenly Clouds Motel took less time than going to Sai Kung, with the traffic counter-flow lighter. They made a casual drive-by. There were no pedestrians. They parked opposite the gates and waited.

Within half an hour, three separate cars with couples aboard entered the motel grounds. Twice, two men chatting together appeared at the gateway then disappeared back inside each time. These were Jonnie Half Moon's protectors, stretching their legs waiting for the girlfriend to re-appear.

At eleven o'clock Jules and Jack made their move. The dim street lighting around the motel was not accidental. The motel management had coated the lights with a darkening blue spray, allowing more privacy for their guests.

The former commandos inserted themselves through the gate and eased to either side, keeping close to the surrounding walls. Toward the rear, the two bodyguards engaged in hushed conversation. The trained ears of the black-clad men picked up the Cantonese twang as the men spoke. In concert, a pincer movement brought them parallel behind the unsuspecting targets.

They didn't need to use their daggers, nor the silenced pistols. A simultaneous armlock and twist took seconds to render each of the sentries lifeless with snapped necks. The dead men sagged to the ground. Jack tried the handle of the Bentley standing in the shadow under the bungalow's side canopy. It opened without a sound. They laid the bodies inside the back of the car and closed the door.

The only noise audible was faint, Chinese music from where Jonnie Half Moon dallied with his lady.

They circled to the rear of the detached building. The main bedroom occupied most of the space. This was not a normal dwelling-house layout. It was an amusement room. The music blared. Through the darkened window they saw two figures in the dim light, lying on a large circular bed. One of the figures rose. A tall lady, naked, made her way to the far corner of the room and disappeared into a curtained opening.

Jules and Jack exchanged glances.

Good.

They listened further. The distinct sound of running water became audible, then faded. She had closed the bathroom door to take a shower.

The intruders prised open the flimsy, back entry and moved stealthily across the bedroom, silenced lugers ready. The music volume increased. Jonnie Half Moon lay naked, face down, with his head toward where Jack Calder approached the bed.

Jack stared. Jonnie was tied up! How good did this get?

Jules covered the door to the bathroom.

Jack glanced toward it. Keep showering lady, keep showering.

He would never know if the Chinese gangster heard Jack's whispered voice above the noise of the sound system.

"The Violin Man's stopped playing, Jonnie boy," he said, as Jonnie raised his head and Jack squeezed gently on the hair-trigger. "And he's not coming back."

The twin had no time to utter a word as a neat bullet hole formed on his forehead above his eyes. The noise of running water continued.

Jules stepped toward the body. Blood oozed from the head wound. From inside his own jacket, Jules removed a folded sheet of paper which he pushed into the mouth of the dead man.

The sound of the shower continued. Perfect.

They retreated the way they had come in. No-one

else witnessed their exit from the compound. Moments later, they turned the car's nose back toward Sai Kung.

* * * * *

Debbie had never seen a corpse before. The sight that met her eyes when she came out of the bathroom left her dumbstruck. But no scream. No terror. Just astonishment. Her mind raced.

What should she do? Call someone? And be found in a bedroom with a dead man? No. Get the hell out as fast as possible. That's what she had to do.

She didn't panic, impressing the heck out of herself. Even with the vision of the paper sticking out of his mouth, she kept calm, knowing not to touch it. She dressed in a hurry, making sure she had her belongings together, leaving nothing behind. She stopped.

He hadn't paid her yet.

Jonnie's wallet lay on top of the dressing table with more cash than she earned in a month. She took it all. She wasn't to know it then, but years later, she would dine out on the story.

She looked back at her dead patron. The blood from the hole in his forehead formed a pattern with the crescent birthmark at the right of his temple.

Almost like a red full moon.

CHAPTER 37

A touch before midnight, the dimmed lights of the car drew near to where May-Ling waited.

Jules approached and spoke first. "Any movement?"

"No-one in, no-one out," she replied. "Only the bodyguards walking around to take a smoke then back together at the white Mercedes."

Her colleagues looked over to where she indicated. They could make out the shape of two figures leaning against the bonnet of the vehicle.

From May-Ling's car they trained the night-vision glasses toward the guards. Next, a criss-cross on the rest of the property. No other personnel visible. The windows remained shuttered as during the morning reconnaissance run. Only partial light covered the ground to where the men were smoking. Ample cover.

"Okay, May-Ling, we're going in now. Keep your eyes peeled in case we need back-up action. I don't expect so, but keep watching and listening," instructed Jules.

"Got it," she replied, as the two men stepped out of the car.

The commandos had the AK47s strapped across their backs. She watched with approval as they glided unhurriedly toward the sentries. As with the guards at Wong Tai Sin, the classic pincer attack was swift and deadly. The bodyguards never knew what hit them. Stilettos sliced their throats, silencing them forever.

Jules approached the corner at the back of the building to check for guards at the rear. None, meaning everyone else was inside. With external bodyguards, Jimmie Chan had no need for locked doors. Good. They entered the front door into a medium-sized hallway. At the end of the hall, the kitchen area abutted an ante-room. They heard voices talking in Cantonese. These were the extra guards. At Jack's signal, Jules and he stepped quietly like shadows into the room and shot two men each through the head, Jack taking a pair on the right, his boss the other two on the left. Clinical. The silencers meant the only sounds made were the bodies sliding to the floor, with one man slumped over the small coffee table in front of him. The tinkling noise of a bell rang from the large room across the hallway.

Someone looking for service.

Jack allowed himself a grin. Coming right up.

They readied the AK47s. Same routine, Jack to the right, Jules to the left. With Jack leading, Jules moved on his nod. A violent kick crashed opened the lounge door to the astonishment of the assembled mahjong players. What the…? Two men in black entered with guns blazing. No silencers required this time. In seconds it was all over. Eight high-ranking triad criminals executed in as little time as it took to make a mahjong call.

Drinks glasses scattered across the tables. Chairs lay where they tipped over, with the falling body weight of dead men. Mahjong tiles and cash littered the floor. Laden ashtrays donating silent palls of smoke offered the only remaining movement in the room. Blood was everywhere. The carnage was intentional. No neat hits. Scattered killing, Chinese triad style.

At the table closer to the door, one face bore the familiar crescent mark on the right cheek. Jimmie Half Moon preceded his brother into the world by minutes and exited not long after his sibling.

Jules removed a second, folded sheet of paper from his jacket and left the same calling card as with Jonnie Chan. The message protruded from the dead man's mouth like a half-posted letter.

May-Ling started the car as her guys returned, checking the highway for unwelcome eyes. Minutes later, they headed back to Tsuen Wan.

CHAPTER 38

Detective Inspector Archie Campbell rang his boss at one-thirty in the morning. He thought to catch him still awake as they'd parted company only an hour earlier. In fact, Donnie Mullen had just fallen asleep. He made his usual gruff coming-out-of-sleep telephone reply, "Who's this?"

"Boss. Archie here. We got a call from the Heavenly Clouds Motel in Wong Tai Sin. One of our favourite Half Moon boys has been taken out."

"What?" Now he was fast awake. "Details, Archie? Details?"

"We've people crawling all over the motel, boss. A Brazilian trannie turned up around midnight. Jonnie Half Moon's a regular client he says. The guy's terrified he's gonna be blamed. Screamed for the motel manager straight away. He called for the police, and a squad car reached the scene at twenty-five minutes after midnight."

"Man, that's a turn-up for the book. What did the lads find?"

"Jonnie's Bentley's in the driveway at the side of the building. The ladyboy says they always used the same villa. Two dead bodies in the rear seat of the car. Bodyguards. Both with broken necks. In the playroom, Jonnie's lying nude, trussed up, a bullet hole in the head."

"Any sign of the girlfriend?"

"No girlfriend. No female clothing. An empty wallet. The shower was used recently. But boss, there's no way the girl did this."

"How do you figure that?"

"This is the best bit. Someone left a love note stuffed in Jonnie's mouth. A very triad style of delivering a message, as you know, boss."

"Go on, I suppose it had this week's racing winners on it?"

Archie chuckled. "The squad car boys called us immediately. I came down with the lads. The note's in Chinese of course."

"What's it say?"

"Burn in hell, Half Moon Pig."

"That's all?"

"There's a sign also. The Mok Kwong Cho."

Donnie whistled. "Well, I'll be damned. Not been their week, eh? Any word from Jimmie Half Moon or anyone else from the Ching Tan Ka?"

"Nothing boss. We've got the prints boys all over the scene. This is a seriously professional hit."

"Ok. Thanks for the call Archie. Get what you can and let's meet at seven in the morning. I'm bushed. I need some of my ugly sleep. Goodnight."

"Good morning," corrected Campbell.

* * * * *

The second interruption to the DCI's sleep came at four o'clock when his number two roused Donnie once more. This time, Archie Campbell couldn't keep his tone down. This was big.

"Unbelievable stuff, boss. Jimmie Chan and seven of his lieutenants have been massacred in Sai Kung."

Donnie was out of bed, already reaching for his shirt.

"Talk to me, Archie."

"We tried to track Jimmie down to ask when he'd last been with his brother. By the time we got round to checking the Sai Kung mahjong address, it was gone three already. All the lights were on. Our lads found two guards outside with their throats slit. Inside was a slaughterhouse. Four more heavies in a side room, pistol shots to the head. In the mahjong lounge, eight guys taken out including Jimmie Chan. The bullet patterns are AK47s. The Mok Kwong Cho use AK47s." Archie paused for breath.

"Anything else?"

"Yes. Jimmie Chan had the same written message stuck in his mouth we found on Jonnie. They never had a prayer. These are the best hits I've ever seen."

"Hmm," said Donnie. "I'm on my way into the office now. Rustle up the first boys on the scene at Wong Tai Sin and Sai Kung to join us. Locate the girl and bring her in. We need to talk to her. Let's get this while it's fresh."

"Right. See you later."

CHAPTER 39

Debbie was startled by insistent knocking at the door of her flat. She blinked at the bedside alarm. Quarter to six. Who the hell? After the horror of the evening last night, she hadn't slept a wink.

A male and a female police officer waited at the doorstep.

"Miss Devlin?" asked the policewoman.

"Yes."

The officer explained she should best come with them to help answer a few questions regarding Mr Jonnie Chan.

Jesus. Now I'm in trouble big time .

At the police station she was shown into a private room. Another female officer and two men in plain clothes awaited her.

"Coffee, Miss Devlin?" asked Archie Campbell.

Good idea. "Yes please." God. They all knew her name.

"Cigarette?"

"No thanks. I don't smoke."

"Miss Devlin, this is Detective Chief Inspector Mullen. I'm Detective Inspector Campbell. You'll notice no tape recorders running. This is an informal chat to begin with. Where we go after that is pretty much up to you. Do you understand?"

"I think so. You want to talk about what happened to Jonnie Chan last night, right?" Her broad Manchester accent filled the room.

"Yes. We'd very much like to get your take on that," replied Archie. "We believe you met with Jonnie earlier in the evening at the Heavenly Clouds Motel?"

"Yes. I did. We went there every Wednesday night. From about nine-thirty until just before twelve. Same routine for a few months now."

"Would you consider yourself his girlfriend?" asked Campbell.

"No. Not a steady girlfriend. Jonnie and I have... er, had, a regular business arrangement. Some fun on Wednesday nights. Nothing in between. I never met him anywhere else except at the club where I work. But normally always at the motel. He had me picked up and taken back afterward, good as clockwork."

The detectives already had all this information, but didn't reveal that to Debbie.

"So, what happened last night? You weren't returned to the club as usual," said the policeman.

"I wish I knew. We did our...we played for a while

like we usually did. Made love a couple of times. I went for a shower. Must have been no more than about fifteen minutes. I finished and came out of the bathroom. He lay on the bed with this mess on his head with the blood. And a silly piece of paper stuck in his mouth."

"No sign of anyone in the room? You didn't hear any noise? No gunshot?"

"Nothing. That's the weird bit. To be honest, I just wanted to get the hell out of the place."

"Did he ever talk about having enemies. People who might want to have a go at him?"

"Never. I don't even know what business he was in," said Debbie. "We get all types of guys coming into the club. Mostly decent people. I've never had a problem with any of my guests in all the time I've been here."

"How long has that been?" asked Campbell.

"I came over from Manchester eight months ago. They got me a proper job at the club, all legal like."

"Didn't anybody talk to you concerning Mr Chan. Who he is? What he does?" continued Archie.

"I knew he had a lot of girls available. Not surprising really. He was a good bloke, always nice to me. Generous into the bargain. That's all I can tell you about him."

"Ah. Generous. You took money from his wallet? It was empty?" queried Archie.

She looked down at the table.

"You took the money from his wallet?" repeated Campbell.

"Yes," she replied in a whisper. "He hadn't paid me. I probably shouldn't have, but…" her voice trailed off.

For the first time the other plain-clothed man addressed her. "But a lady's got to live, right?" said the second detective, obviously the boss.

"I'll give it back," she started.

Donnie Mullen continued, "That won't be necessary, Miss Devlin. For what it's worth, I don't believe for a second you had anything to do with Mr Chan's killing. You are, however, in a very dangerous situation. There will be people who know or who'll get to know you were there when he was shot. They may not believe you had nothing to do with it. That puts your own life at very serious risk."

"My God," she said. "I swear to you I had no part in it."

"As I said, we believe you," replied Donnie. "That's why I want you to listen very carefully and do exactly what I'm about to tell you. If you stay in Hong Kong, the odds on you being killed are extremely high. I've no desire to see another needless death on this patch. As far as I can judge, you've seen nothing and can add nothing to this case as any type of witness. You don't exist, Miss Devlin. Do you hear what I'm saying?"

"I don't think I get you," she replied, puzzled.

"Here's what you're going to do," said Donnie. "This lady officer will accompany you and another of my men to collect your travelling things from your flat. That you'll complete as quickly as possible. Only your travelling things, you understand?"

Debbie nodded.

"There'll be a one-way ticket in your name on the British Airways flight to London just after midday today. My officers will escort you aboard the plane. Wherever you lived in England, you stay away from there for at least three months. After that it should be safe enough for you to move freely around in England as you please. You will never return to Hong Kong. Understood?"

"Yes Mister...Mister?"

"Mullen."

"Yes, Mister Mullen. I understand completely. But why are you...?"

He didn't let her finish. "I said before, we've got enough needless killings around this town, we don't need another one. Goodbye, Miss Devlin."

The big policeman rose and left the room before she could splutter out her thanks.

CHAPTER 40

The Trade Show closed on Thursday evening. The attendance at Gemtec's pavilion ran brisk and constant throughout the entire four days. The attempted hijacking of the gems on the way to the Coliseum was the major talking point of the week and generated more visitors to the stand than normal. Deryk Ostman was astute enough to turn that into a positive public relations opportunity. It wasn't necessary to double the guards at the Gemtec display inside the venue, but he and Jack agreed to do so anyway as an added bit of spice to their presentation. The order book far exceeded achievements from prior years. Ostman invited the ISP team to his suite for a celebratory dinner.

"Your people performed superbly this week, Mr Townsend," he said. "I'm grateful to you. The arrangements at the Show itself were meticulous. Mr Calder's suggestion of the added men was a bit of an eye-catcher. The dreadful incident the other morning, while one would rather it hadn't happened, demonstrated to me the excellent decision to ask you to protect Gemtec's interests. I regret of course the attacks on your Mr McGuire."

"We're pleased you're happy, Mr Ostman. I trust this'll be the first of many successful operations on Gemtec's behalf," replied Jules. "I know you've visited Malky every day, and I can tell you from myself and my team, your concern is appreciated. The reports on him are fair to good. He's in the best place meantime, getting the finest of medical attention. We hope he'll be discharged soon. Now we have to get your merchandize returned to Holland in a timely manner."

"Quite so, Mr Townsend. However, we won't need to send it all back to Amsterdam, only some. The goods are already out of the country, and given the order book during this week, I'd like to discuss with Miss Wong how to organize deliveries to other international centres."

"No problem, Mr Ostman," chimed in May-Ling. "In fact, the logistics are more manageable with smaller aggregate shipments to multiple destinations. I'll need the split shipment manifests from you as soon as it suits you."

"Tomorrow morning, Miss Wong. My marketing division already has the despatch details for me to authorize," he replied with a smile.

* * * * *

As pre-arranged, Donnie Mullen arrived alone to meet with Jules in his room after the dinner engagement with Ostman.

"Someone's done Hong Kong a massive favour," he said. "Lots of vermin taken out of the system last night. Can't say I'd be losing sleep over it. Though I must say, I've had precious little of that since four o'clock this morning."

Jules replied, "What's the take, Donnie?"

"The unofficial version or the official one?" asked Donnie. "The official line, which we're pushing now, is the Mok Kwong Cho boys were getting increasingly pissed at the Half Moons for monopolizing certain slices of the trade. We've the written curses left behind in the mouths of Jonnie and Jimmie pointing to a classic triad take-out. No witnesses to the attacks fits with a gang killing. It's unlikely anybody's going to step up to volunteer eyewitness accounts. The AK47s used are typical triad weapons. Leaving no-one alive is also standard hit practice. There's no evidence to refute our version. No fingerprints. No footmarks. Nothing."

"And the unofficial version?" queried Jules.

"Just between us, Jules?" asked Donnie. He smiled and looked directly at the ISP boss. "If I was being hypothetical, I could give you a scenario where superb professional assassins rendered excellent service to this community we're all trying to clean up."

"Go on," prompted Jules.

"For example, it would be difficult to imagine how the guards at the motel both ended up with broken necks," continued Donnie. "Very careless of them to bump into one another like that. Almost identical to the lads on the landing the other night waiting to take out May-Ling. They also bumped themselves carelessly as I remember."

"Yes, very careless," Jules responded, smiling.

"The pistol shots on the four guys in the room across from the mahjong salon made no noise, otherwise the players would've been alerted," Donnie carried on. "Same as the shot that took out Jonnie at the Heavenly Clouds. I'd hazard a guess from marksmen who don't miss. The knife work on the guards outside the villa in Sai Kung is also not from around these parts. But as I say, all hypothetical, eh?"

"Quite so," responded Jules. "What about Mister Half Moon's young lady friend?"

"If you're referring to the rather splendid Miss Double-D Debbie, she's halfway safely to England as we speak. She's likely to remain invisible for some considerable time. The transvestite from Sao Paulo also considered his health may be better enhanced back in Brazil. He flew out this evening." Donnie looked pleased with the way the case was moving. The official version fitted very well.

"You're covering the bases, Donnie. What happens next?"

"It's started already. A swarm of Fortune Group lawyers are battering down the doors to get legal papers processed against the police. They're claiming we failed to protect several of their executives and associates from the bad guys. Simple to dismiss. A bit less easy is the open warfare likely on the cards now amongst the triad gangs."

"Oh?"

"They'll grab the chance to stake out new territory. With the Half Moon twins gone, everything's up for grabs. One benefit is we'll find a lot more of their front line guys getting hit. Saves us the trouble of having to put them away."

"So, no heartbreak?" half statement, half question.

"None at all. The letter messages was a masterstroke as far as I'm concerned. If I was more of a cynic than I am, I'd put that down to someone as clever as May-Ling Wong."

Jules grinned.

"There's good progress on the cases regarding the documents we took from their offices this week. My guys tell me they've enough evidence already to throw the book at most of their senior people, including some of their fancy lawyers. Dozens, possibly hundreds of smaller operators are due a knock on the door from the Anti Money Laundering boys. We've already shared this with Jens Kluvin. He's in a similar situation. Lots of stuff to keep their businesses closed in Holland for good. A break-through for Jens too, by the way. Mr Choi kept tight-lipped, but Mr Kai was persuaded playing ball with Kluvin could save his skin. He'll be offered witness protection."

"A first-class week for the good guys."

"We need all the breaks we can get against this scum, Jules. Some disappear one day, and next day, more leap out from the lice beds," said Donnie, with feeling.

"It's time for a drink. What do you think?"

"Sure, if ISP's paying, why not?" he laughed.

Jules buzzed Jack's room to ask he and May-Ling to come over and join them. He wasn't the least bit surprised May-Ling was already with him when he called.

"Mister Mullen's in the mood to enjoy our hospitality. Bring a thirst with you," he instructed Jack.

"We'll be right with you," was the loud response.

CHAPTER 41

Jules left May-Ling with precise instructions regarding the continuing care and treatment of Malky McGuire. Jack added his personal orders concerning continued regard for her own safety.

Donnie Mullen met them for some strong, black coffee at the airport lounge before departure. They all nursed various sizes of hangovers from the previous evening. What started as a casual drink in Jules' suite stretched almost until dawn. Time for boarding cut short the farewells. Jack and Jules intended to catch up on their sleep on the way home to London.

* * * * *

The Saturday morning dawn over London hinted at a good day as they descended from a cloud-free sky at Heathrow Airport. Jules' arrangements included a car and driver at the arrivals exit. The limousine met light. early-morning weekend traffic as they headed out towards Stirling Lines barracks at Hereford to meet an old friend in the intelligence sector of the SAS.

The regiment's headquarters complex was familiar ground to them, and Jack felt the home-coming buzz as they entered the gates. Mac waited for them at the parking area. Mac's real name had dissolved long ago into distant memory. The librarian, record keeper, and intelligence guardian for the regiment, he'd filled the role for more than twenty years.

"Hello, Mac. Grand to see you again. How's things?" said Jules as they stepped out of the car.

"Just dandy, Jules. Hello, Jack. Good to have you here," he replied. Mac, a Major himself, had lost the use of his left arm in an incident in Borneo early in his SAS career. The empty sleeve of his tunic was immaculately folded and tucked into the left-hand uniform pocket. Denied further active combat duty after his injury, the regiment had honed his analytical skills and given Mac perpetual charge of the confidential records and intelligence files.

"How you doing with the material I threw at you, Mac? Any luck?" asked Jules.

"Plenty Jules. Come on inside and get a cuppa. I think I've got enough stuff to keep you happy," he replied, leading the pair into an anonymous long-corridored building.

They passed by a succession of bolt-locked doors. No other personnel appeared as they walked along the corridor. The room at the end was open, but as with most of the structures at Stirling Lines, it had no exterior windows.

Mac led the way inside. An automatic drinks server coughed out tea and coffee on demand. Sugar, fresh milk and an opened box of chocolate biscuits lay next to the dispenser.

Laid out on the oblong table in the middle of the room were several neat files with yellow markers attached. Each marker bore a handwritten notation. Mac was the king of this particular castle and his organizational ability was evident from the presentations.

They poured themselves coffee and sat down.

"Okay. Let's get started," Mac said, reaching for a pencilled list at his end of the table.

"First, Hubert Meiss and Nils Bergman," he began. "Rich pickings, gentlemen. Well-known mercenaries in their day. Pretty successful. Hubert always the leader. Been in the Balkans, and Africa. Dabbled a bit with the terroristas in South America. All over the place. Paraguay, Peru, Bolivia and Chile. More of that later. Bergman caught some shrapnel from a grenade he should've dodged somewhere in Bolivia. Meiss got him out in one piece. Two other compadres at the time were not so lucky."

Mac picked up a second file, double-checking the contents.

"Yes. You guys fought on the same side with Meiss, but not with Bergman, in the little jamboree you had in the Congo. Almost the last mission before your demob if I'm not mistaken. Nineteen eighty-two?" queried Mac.

Jack recalled it perfectly. Potentially political dynamite sortie. All squad members deniable as to country and government of origin if captured or killed. Small hit team. Ten men, four of them from the SAS, three from the American Seals and three outsiders coming along for the ride. One of the outsiders was Hubert Meiss. A jungle ambush was planned to take out a corps of torture troops under the wing of the local shadow Minister of Defence. Government ministers from Europe and America negotiated with the Congolese bigwigs in front of the world's television cameras, while the invisible firepower did its job. All the good guys came out alive. None of the torture brigade survived. A ruthless hit. Jack remembered how effectively Meiss and his two mercenaries performed.

"Now Jules, to the core of what you're looking for," continued Mac. "Back to Chile and Bolivia. Both these guys know the terrain well. There's a bit of a story to tell you. This'll give you a better picture of it." Mac laid out a couple of his sheets and proceeded to enlarge the scenario for them.

Mac wore all the hallmarks of a good college professor. He took his former colleagues through the information in the manner of a scholastic dissertation.

"You probably know a lot of this already, guys, but let me try to put it in some context for you," Mac began. "In the late seventies and early eighties there was explosive growth of the cocaine drug trade all across South America. The coca plant became the symbol as a key to cheat poverty for farmers and peasants living on the survival line. As usual, the smart guys and hoodlums who fed off them were the cartel organizers. Some bigger than others, but they all competed to force-feed the world's demand for the drug. Rival organizations structured along military lines sprung up all over the continent. Multi-million dollar shipments of cocaine, raw and refined, moved across borders. Sometimes in a series of small deliveries, often in larger loads. Well-armed guards always accompanied the latter. Turf wars proliferated. Life was purchased through guns and enforcers. Conscience was non-existent. Into this mix came the hired mercenaries. Killers for hire. Protectors of shipments. The instant money for these men was good. Delivery made, or executions complete, cash on the nail. No formal price list existed, but most of the cartel gangs settled at around the same payment levels for the mercenaries' service."

The intelligence man looked at Jules who nodded for him to continue.

"Your chums, Meiss and Bergman, arrived on the continent along with a couple of other soldiers of fortune and began to build a modest reputation for reliability. The quartet was always reasonable in demands for payment quotas. They figured not being too greedy meant repeat engagements. At the time, the right operators enjoyed an endless stream of business, The regular area they worked covered the north of Chile, all the way into the Bolivian capital, La Paz. In Chile, the staging post was the northern town of San Pedro de Atacama."

Jules and Jack peered at the map where Mac pointed.

"Several run-lines straddled across the Andes through the more remote mountain routes," he went on. "This made it easier to identify any unwelcome presence.

Corruption was a way of life for most elected officials on both sides of the border. Loyalties were indexed directly to the dollar. The four mercenary lads comprising Hubert's group maintained a low profile. They ferried their masters' product well and kept their mouths shut. Their drug deliveries habitually landed safely in the correct hands. Like all good things however, nothing lasts for ever." Mac chuckled. "Jealousies over kickback payments at levels above their paymasters produced ambushes at regular intervals. It was only a matter of time before things turned sour. One evening in June, which is the height of sticky summer in these parts, close to a staging rest-post on the Bolivian side of the border, Meiss and his men were attacked. The fire-fight left most of the couriers dead. Nils Bergman took shrapnel from a grenade explosion. A nearby jeep bore the brunt of the blast, but the deflected wave caught him below the knee. He still carries tiny pieces of the metal in his left leg. The other two mercenaries lost their lives in the same explosion. Meiss dragged Bergman away from the carnage, shooting cover fire and saving himself and his partner. Not so the drug shipment. Meiss would never learn how much value they lost, as they were never informed how much they protected on any run. The paymasters above ordered the execution of the intermediary handler. Meiss and Bergman reckoned it was time for them to leave South America until things cooled down. They've not returned to the area since," he concluded, patting the files like a schoolmaster would encourage a child to 'run along'.

Jack never questioned Mac as to how and where he got the information. It was always reliable.

"That explains the leg limp on Bergman," he said. "Tough nut, Hubert Meiss. He performed well in the Congo, too."

"I wouldn't doubt it," replied Mac.

"I don't suppose the names of the other two guys who died were Philip Jacoob and Jon Vogel?" he asked the intelligence officer.

"Ah. Philip Jacoob and John Vogel," Mac continued. "You're familiar with these boys already. They're undercover names for Meiss and Bergman."

"How can you be sure?"

Mac smiled and lifted another file towards him. He extracted more papers. "Here," he said, stabbing his finger on a couple of familiar faces on the sheets in front of him.

Staring out in the vacant, passport photograph way that never truly captures what the sitters look like were the head and shoulders shots of Meiss and his number two, Bergman. Passports in the names of Philip Jacoob and John Vogel.

Jules addressed Mac, "As expected, Mac, eh? How about signatures? Any luck on them?"

Jack wondered how much of this intelligence Jules

had pre-thought and then had Mac do the research. He had only asked his boss to check out a couple of names. This was a whole different class of information.

"The difficult we do immediately," Mac smiled. "The impossible takes a little longer."

He held up two white sheets with several copies of the same writing on them.

"Here's the signatures," he said. "They were on the false passports. We've blown them up and enhanced them a bit. Perfectly legible. Perfectly usable."

"You're a magician, Mac. A bloody magician," replied Jules, nodding approval. "How about the other things I asked?"

What other things? Jack wondered.

"Yes. Got them also. Lists of demolition companies near San Pedro de Atacama. Three of them. A lot of government road reconstruction in progress now. Names of the project guys in charge of each of them, with telephone numbers. You're all set with these. My best contact man down there will greet you in Calama. His name's Rico. Anything you need on the Chile side, he can help you with. He's free-lance, but a hundred percent reliable. Runs with our American cousins from time to time. He'll also have the package for you."

"Excellent," said Jules.

What package? This was the first direct intimation to Jack they were heading for South America.

"Names of a couple of police chiefs in La Paz," continued Mac. "One we only heard of recently. Not much to leverage on. The other one's already long on the file. Survivor by the sniff of him. He's your more likely candidate. General Javier de Santos. Late fifties. He'll have stuff on every criminal activity in the last thirty years in and around La Paz, and should do nicely. Runs a big mansion, top of the range cars, own bodyguards, the usual scene," gestured Mac.

"Right," replied Jules. "Now where do we look for accommodation in San Pedro de Atacama?"

Jules really does take this stuff personally.

"Got you reservations in the Taverna del Tatio. Named after a famous local geyser field," the intelligence guru replied. "You should be able to remember the name. You're tourists, lots of great sand flats to go point your cameras at."

As Mac handed Jules an envelope he said, "Tickets here, invoice to ISP as instructed. Expenses for Rico will be billed as usual after the event." He also handed over a larger package containing copies of all the details already shared with them.

"Magnificent, Mac. Dinner on me in London," announced Jules.

The former commandos shook hands with their ex-colleague before heading back toward London.

"How does Mac keep all this stuff running around in his head?" asked Jack. "How many staff does he have?"

"One. Himself. He says he knows who to blame if he screws up. I've yet to find him even coming close to being wrong. He's a one-off. You can stake your life on his information being right. A lot of other people do."

"Understood. I thought we'd wiped out enough flying this week, boss. When're we off again?"

"Flight this afternoon at six-ten. LAN Airlines to Santiago. We'll be about a whole day in the sky, so buy a good book at the airport."

"You gonna share this thinking stuff with me at some stage, Mr Townsend?" said Jack, laughing back at his boss.

"Certainly Mr Calder. All in due time. On the plane'll be soon enough. Now let's go find a decent restaurant for lunch."

CHAPTER 42

The morass of paperwork taken from the Fortune offices in Holland and Hong Kong sorted into manageable streams of information. The prosecution's accounting professionals separated steady-state, normal business from the documents relating to offshore items requiring closer investigation. They knew what to look for.

Jens Kluvin and Donnie Mullen conversed several times daily, coordinating the progress reports from the respective accounting teams. Within two days of the office raids, the number crunchers in Europe and Asia started to correlate specific threads of payments.

The offshore vehicles in British Virgin Islands, Dutch Antilles and the Channel Islands appeared with almost monotonous regularity. Matching entries occurred enabling the joint forces to state with accuracy siphoned, offshore payments, through which particular Fortune subsidiary, and the remittance beneficiaries. Only a small portion of these went to Nils Bergman's account.

Nils received a continuous payment stream stretching back more than three years. Many other names were credited large and regular monies. Over the period, a staggering sum of no less than six hundred million dollars coursed through the offshore banks.

This provided the explanation for the question that had puzzled Kluvin.

With over two and a half million dollars in Bergman's Banque Roche & Wilhelm account, if it hadn't come from diverting value from Gemtec, then from where?

The bulk of the funding flows in and out of the offshore accounts summarized as drug proceeds. It became clear the business tentacles of the Chans reached through most of Europe where the Ching Tan Ka operated, with Amsterdam a primary centre for the trans-shipments across the rest of the continent as well as the conduit for the Asian shipments.

The confirming element came from Mr Kai, the operations head for Alliance Trading. Under the offer of immunity from charges and protection from the Dutch authorities for his evidence as a state witness, the day after his arrest he began to direct the detectives through the structure of finance, shipments and drug sourcing.

Nils Bergman was pivotal as the brains and coordinator for all of the logistics as the various consignments ferried to their outlets. The covering umbrella of Gemtec's legitimate business provided Bergman a stable and unimpeachable means for the movement of the drugs. The standing arrangements with Customs enabled swift and effortless import facilitation for the gem company's own consignments. Shipments routed in the first instance to other Fortune-related companies in the country to offload the contraband before completion of legitimate deliveries. Ostman never questioned any element of the process as Gemtec's goods always reached their delivery points on time.

This explained the commission payments steadily mounting in Bergman's private bank account.

The hits on the gold and diamond deliveries symptomized a growing greed on the part of the Chans. Requirement for extra immediate cash. No more, no less. Even the clever guys make mistakes.

The dossier of related entities began to take shape. Company names, some of them familiar trading firms in their respective countries, were identified. Frankfurt, Copenhagen, Zurich, London, Brussels, Paris and Moscow figured prominently. This was a massive coup.

Jens and Donnie organized conference calls with their counterparty Chiefs of Police in these centres in order to move quickly before the local operations disappeared completely. The smarter operators already closed shop after the whiff of the first raids, but many would be caught. By the end of the third day after the interventions in Holland and Hong Kong, the authorities mounted a complex operation across Europe. Multi-forces cooperation targeted a simultaneous swoop on more than one hundred and forty addresses.

In each centre, as with the initial targets in Rotterdam, Amsterdam and Hong Kong, noisy and public arrests provided as much newspaper coverage as possible, intended as a body blow from which the Fortune Group drug network would never recover.

Kai didn't pin Hubert Meiss to the criminal activity, but Jens Kluvin was convinced the German and Bergman had been an inseparable team, with Nils doing the thinking work. Hubert acted as a shield for his activities from inside Gemtec, and from Deryk Ostman. The detectives received from Kai another name, a lower level employee within Bergman's office, also involved in processing a major part of the paperwork. They'd missed the man on the first screening for possible insiders. He also agreed to become a state witness in return for the promise of a reduced sentence.

The severity of the police impact on the group's empire increased and the flood of legal cases attacking the authorities in Holland and Hong Kong receded. The lawyers drawn in to represent the Fortune Group began to disassociate themselves from a business they now considered criminal.

The newspapers had a field day.

Kluvin and Mullen finished their telephone call on the evening of the Europe-wide raids, and enjoyed the satisfaction that comes too rarely for law enforcement personnel.

One to the good guys.

Donnie Mullen wondered how Jules and Jack were faring.

CHAPTER 43

The former commandos discussed various action options on the flight to South America. Jack understood his boss was on a mission to balance the books. Meiss and Bergman figured directly or indirectly in the deaths of at least three innocent people in the past several weeks, including a former buddy in the person of Securimax's Roddie Bell.

That was personal.

Furthermore, by attacking Gemtec's shipments, this constituted a direct assault on ISP's business. Jules Townsend's business.

That was even more personal.

The double hit on Malky McGuire was truly family.

That was deeply, deeply personal.

The entire reason for ISP's existence espoused specialist security for high value product clients, and the protection of life. The two mercenaries had crossed the line and now loomed in the crosswire sights of the former commando chief. Jack knew the hunted men would be allowed neither rest nor sanctuary once Jules had the bit between his teeth. He guessed these men were also aware of that.

This part of South America was unfamiliar territory for the ISP men. Jules had seen action in Cuba before

Jack joined the SAS. Both had French and Spanish as semi-working languages, something encouraged in their specialist units, with Jules by far the more fluent.

Nothing had been uncovered in Holland by Jens Kluvin in the past couple of weeks to hint at the specific whereabouts of the former Gemtec executives. The working theory was each had driven crossborder to different airports and used their cover identities to fly to Chile. Without the ability to pinpoint which departure points, it was almost impossible to track them down quickly. Jens pulled in favours from neighbouring countries' police forces to check airline passenger lists. The lack of confirmation of exact dates made the task difficult and slow. Jules had decided to proceed to San Pedro de Atacama and work on it from there.

The long flight from London gave them ample opportunity to catch up on sleep. By the time Arturo Merino Benitez Airport came into view in Santiago, they itched to get off the plane. The next leg of the trip meant a flight to a domestic airstrip in the north of the country at the town of Calama, about a hundred miles from San Pedro de Atacama. Passport and customs formalities entering at Santiago were painfully laboured. Jules tendered his travel document to the immigration officer. The man took a long time to pore through the pages containing previous countries' entry stamps.

"You have been in Cuba and Honduras, Senor?" he asked.

"Yes," replied Jules. "Government engineering contracts."

"And purpose of visit to Chile?"

"Same thing, senor. Road construction up north. We're seeing local officials tomorrow morning."

"Si, Senor. Thank you, and welcome to Chile," he said, handing back his passport.

The kitbags checked in at Heathrow took almost an hour to appear on the baggage carousel. With another three hours to kill before the connecting flight to Calama, the delay mattered little. A cafeteria in the domestic terminal produced some surprisingly good coffee.

The small propeller-driven plane to Calama had seen much better days. Jack recalled flying in similar aircraft in the depths of the African continent. However, flight duration promised less than three and a half hours to travel the fifteen hundred or so miles from Santiago.

Let's hope the weather's good, at least.

The departure schedule bore no resemblance to the time the plane took off, an hour and three-quarters late. Thankfully for Jack, the sun kept the sky free of clouds all the way to Calama. No clouds meant less turbulence and a chance of keeping his stomach from flipping over. Flying was not his favourite means of transport. The trip remained smooth, although the patchy, tarmac landing-strip provided more than a few bumps before the chocks were stuck under its front wheel. It felt better with his feet back on the ground. Because of the lighter flying traffic at the small airfield, their baggage unloaded for pick-up about fifteen minutes after landing. As they approached the exit doors, a casually-dressed figure came towards them and spoke to Jules.

"Mr ISP?" he asked.

"Yes," replied Jules.

"My name is Rico. Mac says welcome to Chile, Senor. If you will follow me, I have transport waiting for you," he added with a broad grin.

Good old Mac, thought both men as they looked across their host at each other. Service with a smile, indeed.

"I'm Jules, and this is Jack."

"My pleasure to meet you, Senor."

Rico led them to a jeep parked a hundred yards from the exit, next to a sign that forbade parking.

"We're heading for Taverna del Tatio, Senor, in San Pedro de Atacama, no?" he queried.

"Taverna del Tatio it is, Rico. Gracias."

It didn't take long into their journey, with Rico pumping the accelerator pedal, to register that hammering at full throttle was the primary mode for most drivers on the route to San Pedro de Atacama.

This guy must've had driving lessons from May-Ling, thought Jack.

The jeep hustled its way past other vehicles on the highway. Their guide spoke little on the journey. He seemed more intent on getting his charges to their destination in a new speed record.

The township of San Pedro de Atacama is not a magnet for the tourist seeking luxury or comfort. It nestles in the northern region of the driest desert in the world, the Atacama. Volcanic rock surface and mountain ranges surround the town to each of its wider horizons. Access into its neighbour, Bolivia, is across the Andes range at some of its highest points. The hardier breed of backpacking traveller takes almost masochistic pleasure in traversing the region in old buses with little or no air conditioning other than open windows. Rico's driving didn't fit with sight-seeing.

Close to midtown sat the Taverna del Tatio, a modest hotel, more akin to a boarding house. Paint was a stranger to the exterior and interior walls. The two-storey building held a dozen rooms for rent, with a small dining-room to the side of the foyer.

The Chilean assisted with the formalities of checking-in.

"Two hundred US dollars in advance for three nights covers both of you," he advised them as he handed over the key. "Shared room I'm afraid. The hotel's full of tourists. Meals are extra, Senor Jules. I'll join you in a few minutes."

"Thank you, Rico," said Jules as they headed up the wooden stairway to the first floor.

The room was plain, but clean, the twin beds small and hardly comfortable for the frame of each of the former soldiers. They had slept in conditions much rougher than these. Jules threw his kitbag onto the bed as Rico knocked at the door and reappeared.

He carried a long, black, cloth bag which he placed beside the ISP men's luggage. The package Mac had referred to. Jules opened the bag and Jack watched as his partner extracted several smaller packages, each wrapped in fresh canvas.

The first held Mauser pistols. The second, silencers. The next, rounds of ammunition. A couple of Gurkha-style kukri knives in slim leather sheaths. Complete sets of hand weaponry. The two professionals close-inspected each piece, then handed it over to the other to repeat the exercise.

Detail, detail, detail.

Rico watched them in silence, impressed. These hombres were the real business. The last parcel contained familiar equipment. Detonator-trigger devices and a small radio transmitter.

"Excellent," breathed Jules. "Mac never fails to impress."

"Everything in order, Senor Jules?" asked Rico.

"Couldn't be better, my friend," responded the Englishman. "Couldn't be better. Now, we have some other arrangements to look after. We're going to need your help."

"Tell me, amigo. What do you want?"

Jules began to outline the requirements to their newly-found fixer.

* * * * *

Jules had no assurance Meiss and Bergman were even in the area of San Pedro de Atacama and reckoned the only place for these guys to be meant following their money. The first payment came to the bank here in San Pedro. So here they would start the search.

"It's too small a town for Jack and I to walk around without risking being seen first," said Jules.

"I understand, Senor," replied Rico. "I won't take long to find them, and where they're staying."

"In the meantime, check out the car sales outlets, vehicles suitable for crossing the mountains into Bolivia," said Jules. "Can't be too many in this town."

"You wanna buy a car?"

"Maybe, but let's flush out our boys first. Here's the face shots of Meiss and Bergman," he continued, handing the sheets to Rico. "Find out if they've bought a vehicle and how recently."

"Okay. What else?"

"Here's the names of the guys in charge of the local construction projects. All of these outfits have stores of plastic explosives. We'd like enough to fill about three cigarette packets. This should be ample to persuade one of them to lose a little of their stock with no questions asked," he added, handing over an envelope with a wad of hundred dollar bills.

"Most of them use Semtex. Will that do?" asked the Chilean.

"Plenty good enough," intervened Jack. Now he could see where this was leading. It also explained the absence of any long-arm weapons. No need for them when you plant the plastic kiss.

"Fine," said Jules. "Let's eat, I'm hungry."

The menu in the small downstairs restaurant was all Spanish food, which they attacked with relish.

* * * * *

Rico drew a blank in the first car showroom. No sales in the last week, business slow, complained the owner. The man was hardly a pulsating salesman. No doubt contributing to his no-sales sheet.

A few streets further down from the hotel, the second stop came up trumps.

"Si, Senor. I sold a Land Rover to this hombre two days ago," said the manager of the garage cum sales lot. Used four-wheel drive jeeps and Land Rovers spilled across the front of the outlet, not a market for brand-new models. He pointed to the photograph of Nils Bergman. "He walked with the heavy leg, no?"

"Si, si, amigo. He has a bad leg as you say," responded Rico, pushing a hundred dollar bill into the man's receptive fist. "Was this man with him when he bought?" The shot of Meiss brought no recognition.

"No, Senor. Only the first hombre. An older man, about sixty, no?"

"How did he pay?" asked Rico.

"Dollars cash. He had a small case with him with plenty more dollars inside. He insisted I overhaul the car as he needed to cross to Bolivia soon. He didn't want to get stuck up in the mountains. It took me about three hours to service. He paid extra cash."

"Thank you, amigo. You've been helpful. If I need to buy another car the same from you, you have something available now?"

"Sure," the man replied. "I've two more for sale at the back of the lot. Good condition. I do all the maintenance myself. People around here, they don't treat their cars with respect. You know, like your mother, you treat her bad, she won't look after you. You treat her nice, hey, the sun keeps shining, no? For you I make a good price. You pay dollars cash too, no?"

"Let me come back to you, amigo. Did this guy leave an address in San Pedro?"

"No, he didn't, Senor, but he was walking, and with the heavy leg, I reckon he'd be staying close to here. Most likely place is the guest house two streets down on the right hand side. No name on the outside, but next door to the Alhambra taverna. Green painted walls. You can't miss it."

"Gracias. Adios."

The man hadn't asked if Rico was from the police. The grease money and prospect of another sale were enough to encourage his full cooperation.

* * * * *

The site manager at the civil works on the outskirts of the town looked at his guest. His office in a small make-up shack afforded them privacy to talk. During his career across the South American continent, the request was a familiar one. This polite gentleman required a little blasting explosive to clear away debris in front of the new home he was building on the other side of town. The

Chilean explained he understood the official channels he should go through, but they take such a long time don't they? Paperwork's a nuisance, no? The guest indicated of course he would be grateful for the construction man's help. The open envelope displayed a sheaf of dollar bills. A simple decision. The manager asked Rico to take a short walk with him to the depot.

Once inside, he closed the door and bolted it. He approached another large, locked, tin case and took his keys to the padlock. The man controlled the plastic explosives stocks and didn't have to explain to anyone how much he used in the road works.

"How much blasting do you intend to do, Senor?" he asked. "You said a small amount would serve your needs?"

"At most, half a kilo."

The construction man removed a block of the material, already tightly packed.

"How much did you say this was worth to you, Senor?"

"A thousand dollars should cover it," Rico replied.

"Two thousand has a better sound to it, amigo."

"Okay, two thousand," he responded without missing a beat.

The man wrapped the Semtex in a waterproof sheet and secured it with thick, black tape. He handed the parcel with both hands to his guest.

"Be careful, Senor," he said. "I presume you know how to handle this. We wouldn't want to hear of any accidents. You understand this is a one-time only visit. The company is strict about returning visitors. This is a private project."

"Agreed, amigo. This will meet my needs. Gracias," returned Rico.

He counted out two thousand dollars from his envelope. The money disappeared into the folds of the man's shirt, not the first transaction of this kind he had ever done. Rico wrapped his own linen jacket around the purchase and bid his host goodbye.

The beauty of Semtex is that it's safe to transport, and odourless. Furthermore, it can only be exploded with the use of a detonator. The kind of detonator delivered to Jules Townsend and Jack Calder in the Taverna del Tatio.

* * * * *

His new companions were pleased to hear of his successes as Rico explained his afternoon's progress. The dollars Nils used to pay for the car were no doubt part of the sixty-five thousand sent to the local bank here in San Pedro de Atacama. It all made sense.

Except, where the hell had Meiss gone while Bergman shopped for the vehicle?

"I think we should go visit the guest house next to the Alhambra," said Jules. "Check if our birds are still here, or if they've already started towards the border."

* * * * *

The taverna was twenty minutes walk from the Taverna del Tatio. Jack welcomed the exercise. A cooler breeze accompanied the darkened, evening sky. They dressed in their usual black, night-time clothing, less likely to stand out and be recognized on a chance look from Hubert or Nils. The ISP men waited at the corner of the street and Rico went ahead into the guesthouse. After a short while he returned.

"They still have a shared room, amigos. Paid in advance in dollars for another week. Names of Jacoob and Vogel. Bergman left the place alone in the Land Rover earlier today, before we arrived in town. Meiss hasn't been seen for a day or two. Maybe still in the hotel. Or gone ahead to Bolivia, more likely."

"You looked after the reception people?" queried Jack.

"Si, Senor Jack, dollars talk in this part of the world. Only one man on the desk. It's a small business. Tips are hard to come by. My friend on duty will eat well for another week." He winked. "We can go in now if you want." He handed Jack a key with a wooden tab attached. Room 109.

Jack laughed. "You're a wizard, Rico."

"Right," said Jules. "Time to move. Rico, you stay outside and watch the street. Wait here until we get back, ok?"

"Si, Senor, no problem. Good luck."

CHAPTER 44

The reception area in the guesthouse was deserted except for a middle-aged man in a brown and dark-green, striped jacket standing behind the front desk. Rico's new friend. He hardly glanced at Jules and Jack as they passed by and up the stairs to the first floor.

On the landing, they took a few seconds to identify the door handle halfway down with the 'Do Not Disturb' sign posted outside. Room 109. No-one else in sight.

They withdrew their silenced Mausers. Jack inserted the key into the lock and turned. Noiseless. He eased the door open, holding the handle in one hand, the pistol in the other. Not a sound from inside. No television. No radio. They entered quickly and silently from the hallway. No sign of anyone. A small bathroom to the left side was visible through the open doorway. Nobody home.

In a simple routine they scanned the room with professional eyes. No litter in the ashtray on the coffee table. No used glasses or cups. No discarded clothing lying on any of the furniture. No papers or documents on top of the small table.

In the bathroom, some shaving equipment on the glass shelf. One toothbrush. No toothpaste.

One toothbrush?

And why leave the 'Do Not Disturb' sign on the door?

Jack moved across to the clothes cupboard, gun at the ready. He gingerly turned the handle to access the cupboard. Neither he nor Jules expected what happened next.

Hubert Meiss appeared.

They understood instantaneously the reason for the 'Do Not Disturb' sign

The German was dead. His body rolled sideways from the cupboard where it had offered company to a khaki-coloured kitbag and some soiled clothing.

A dark mass of dried, clotted blood covered one side of his face. Jules approached the bed and drew back the top covering blanket. The pillow and sheets underneath were massively stained. Hubert Meiss had been executed as he slept. Probably with a silenced pistol shot.

"No honour among thieves," Jules said. "Nils Bergman's on a solo run."

They retraced their steps and locked the door, touching nothing else in the room, least of all the dead man. Bergman would not be returning either. He was following the money, the next logical stop the bank in La Paz. So far Jules' predictions for each step had been correct, except the unexpected killing of Meiss. They used to have a term for that. Collateral damage.

As they tracked back towards Rico, Jack threw the hotel key into a nearby garbage can. No fingerprints.

"Meiss is dead," Jules informed Rico. "Good idea to give the guest house a wide berth. We'd like to go purchase the Land Rover you told us about. Will he still be open for business?"

"Si, Senor. In fact, I think he'll be expecting me. It's not too far to walk. Only a couple of streets."

* * * * *

Jack and Jules waited outside while Rico negotiated the purchase of the Land Rover. No need for servicing, he told the manager. It looks roadworthy enough. Dollars cash. No receipt required. Just ensure a full tank of fuel. He also asked the man for licence plate details of the one sold to Bergman. The salesman wrote down the number. "It's a dark-green model," he said. "Somebody put a couple of big dents in the back fender. The previous owner reversed too fast into an iron railing causing a lot of paint damage. I didn't have enough time sort it out for the buyer before he left, so I gave him a discount. If he comes back, I can fix it for him."

"I'll remember," said Rico. "Gracias, amigo."

Jack drove the car back to the Taverna del Tatio. It handled alright. A little wobbly on the steering, but nothing unmanageable.

In their room, they reverted to the material Mac had given them in Hereford. Several means existed to traverse the Andes on the journey to La Paz. Some served the recognizable tourist routes. They discarded them in favour of the old routes used by the drug traffickers. Hubert's dead body may be discovered at any time and Jules figured Nils would prefer the remoter crossings. Pursuit by law enforcement authorities was not a given, but why would he take the chance?

The more likely roads traced the border northward for two hundred and fifty miles. The crossing favoured in the past by mercenaries babysitting the drug loads passed through the mountains at a place known as El Col del Isole. The Lonely Pass.

"We'll head for there," determined Jules. "We start immediately. He can't have more than a half-day ahead of us. My guess is when it gets dark, he'll find some place to rest over until morning. If we start now, we'll make up a fair bit of ground. Rico, we leave you here, amigo."

"But, Senor, I …" the Chilean started to protest.

"No Rico, Your help has been magnificent already," interrupted the Englishman. "I want you out of this area as soon as possible. When the whistle blows on Meiss in the guest house, the only face the concierge is likely to remember is yours. The same with the guy at the garage. It's time for you to disappear. I know Mac'll be looking after your payment, but take this from Jack and I as a small thank you."

Jules handed Rico a packet with a bundle of dollars inside.

"I can't accept, Senor Jules. Mac…"

"Never mind about Mac," said Jules with finality. "That's personal from us. I hope we get to work together again some time. Thanks for everything." He ushered Rico from the room.

* * * * *

With Rico gone, they placed the maps across the table and began to overlay the route in bright, red, marker ink. Part of the way rated class one roadway, the balance less friendly.

They stowed their kitbags in the rear of the Land Rover and left the room key on the coffee table. No need to announce their departure, but they copied Bergman's trick with the 'Do Not Disturb' sign. Having paid in advance, their absence wouldn't be noticed for at least another two days. By then, they'd be long gone into Bolivia.

They tracked the signposts out of San Pedro de Atacama. The road lighting did not stretch far beyond the town limits. In the darkness, however, the lights of the car guided them out toward the Bolivian boundary. The nearest border crossing sat less than an hour and a half driving from the town, but it wasn't their chosen route. Twenty miles from the border, Jack steered the car sharply toward the north, running parallel with the sporadic signage pointing across into Bolivia.

They guessed Bergman's head start at six or seven hours of daylight driving. They also figured he would rest up somewhere en route. With the quieter, evening traffic compared with the heavier flow during the daytime when the Norwegian started, they reckoned to catch him up within another five hours. Jack hit the accelerator pedal and kept as fast a pace as he could on these roads. Jules checked for any possible stopping points along the way, but there were none for the first four hours of the trip.

Jack wasn't the least bit tired. He hadn't welcomed the enforced resting of the last couple of days. Now, back in the field, the old adrenaline spike resurfaced. The road led them higher and higher up the Andes. Sandy, volcanic dust billowed up from the rear wheels of any vehicle they overtook on the way north. Nothing had overtaken them for more than two hours. The evening lapsed into early morning, and even fewer vehicles passed them from the on-coming direction. Jack read the first road-sign for El Col del Isole. Forty miles ahead. Somewhere soon, Bergman must be resting up. Minutes later Jules signalled for his partner to slow down.

A plain, wooden placard with a badly-drawn arrow indicated a rest house area beyond the next turning. Jack brought the Land Rover to a halt about fifty yards into a slip-road leading towards a barn-sized building. The rest house had a fluorescent light over the front door to the building with no other lights visible. A few vehicles parked outside in a dirt-covered parking area. Jack turned off the engine and the lights. The two of them got out of the Land Rover and walked cautiously toward the parking area. At the end nearer to their own vehicle, a dark-green Land Rover was parked. Jules removed from his pocket the piece of paper with the license plate number Rico had given him. He handed it to Jack, who crept toward the rear of the vehicle, the gun already in his left hand. Jules stood cover ten yards back with Jack's own body almost invisible in the darkness. No need to take chances. Bergman had killed once already in the last couple of days. Two and a half million dollars counted reason enough for him to kill again. Through the back window of the Land Rover, Jack could see no-one inside. Back and front seats empty. No kitbag. Bergman intended to sleep in the rest house until the morning light arrived. He replaced the Mauser inside his jacket and opened the sheet with the license number, comparing it with the plate on the back of the car. The number didn't match. He motioned for Jules to join him.

"Number's not the same," he said in a whisper. "Hold on," he continued, flipping his small flashlight onto the rear fender. "There's the two big dents that Rico described. You couldn't mistake them." He felt around the plate screws. They had been changed.

"Clever, Mr Bergman. Just in case he had any lawmen following him. Changed to another set of plates," he whispered to Jules.

"You're right. Okay, let's get some work done while people are still sleeping."

Jack returned to the jeep and retrieved the package wrapped in waterproof paper. They had done this in practice and in real situations many times before. Jack compressed the Semtex into a sandwich-sized parcel. The detonator affixed at one end with the timer and coded radio-signal receiver attached to it. Three small lengths of wire wound around the package. He secured the payload on top of the fuel tank. Totally invisible. Totally lethal. Jules double-checked the installation of the plastic explosive. Satisfied, they retreated to their own vehicle. Jack reversed slowly back along the approach road. They journeyed on for half a mile until they found the vantage point they sought.

Above the main highway, a narrow slip-pathway led up into a cluster of trees which allowed them to see the highway thirty yards below. They could see without being seen. Anyone travelling along the way they had just travelled would be unaware of the observers. Perfect. Time to take alternative watch. Each dozed intermittently until the dawn broke spectacularly across the Andes. They were both wide awake and alert. Their coffee flask and some chocolate bars provided an early breakfast. No sign yet of any passing Land Rover. They didn't have long to wait.

An hour into the daylight, the sound of an engine alerted them to an approaching vehicle. The dark-green Land Rover drove past below them. From their vantage spot, Nils Bergman's distinctive skull was clearly visible behind the driving wheel. A cloud of dust trailed the vehicle as it disappeared around the corner seventy yards ahead. They counting off a full ten minutes and started to tail their quarry. The road in this part of the mountains climbed sharply. The surface offered frequent potholes and gravel scattered across the route. Jack had adjusted to the slight pull to the steering wheel and kept a steady pace behind the Norwegian. The signs to El Col Del Isole guided them upwards and to the left of the roadway.

The openness of the highway gave way to true mountain-pass driving. The terrain reluctantly allowed the road to skewer around its contours. In most places there was no room for two vehicles to pass each other. Regular passing areas were carved into the mountain along the way, effectively a single-lane road. On the right-hand side of the route out of Chile and into the Bolivian mountainside, steep precipices drew the eyes far down to the valley floor. Normal traffic would never choose this dangerous route. Jack reduced the speed. He had no desire to end their trip at the bottom of a rockface.

After travelling for almost an hour, Bergman's vehicle began to appear intermittently about a mile or so in front of them. His Land Rover twisted around the coil of road space up and around the mountain. High speed was impossible, even if he saw them and suspected he was being followed. They thought that unlikely. By the look of it, Nils Bergman was taking his time to traverse the route safely. Ahead, on a hairpin curve in the road, they spotted a break about a mile distant where his vehicle would come into view again. This would serve their purpose. They stopped the car in the next passing area to wait for his re-appearance. After a few minutes, the Land Rover reappeared, moving at a slow pace away from them around the narrow stretch.

"Now's as good a time as any," said Jules. "Detonate."

Jack pointed the transmitter on the hand-held radio towards the Norwegian's car and pressed the send button. One and a half seconds later the receiver under the Land Rover caught the signal. The detonator activated in the Semtex. A huge fireball erupted from under the vehicle. The flame and smoke raced upward against the side of the rockface before leaping outwards along with the car. They saw the flash a second or two before the noise of the explosion carried across the distance to reach their ears.

The blast from the bomb ricocheted off the mountain wall. The already disintegrating car was thrown completely away from the roadway. It bounced and battered in froglike leaps down the perpendicular precipice. From that distance, it almost appeared to be falling in slow motion. The passenger door swung open like a flailing scarecrow's arm and ripped away on the first bouncing collision with the cliff face. Pieces of the Land Rover scattered all the way down the mountainside. No-one was likely to come to collect the debris. No second explosion came, but tongues of fire licked at the frame of the shattered remnants. The smoke thickened, as the tyres started to burn. Nils Bergman was accounted for.

"And then there were none," remarked Jules solemnly. "Let's move, Jack. We've a lot of driving to do yet."

As they passed the explosion spot, only some scorch marks smeared the mountain wall. No vehicle parts remained on the roadway. This part of the job was done.

CHAPTER 45

Jack continued down into Bolivia at a much gentler driving pace. The mountain tracks broadened into roads with two-way lanes. They drove through ample dust clouds from which only a rain-burst would offer any reprieve. A roadside stall provided a hearty meal, enough to carry them all the way to the capital, La Paz.

Traffic remained light, the major means of transport an endless procession of dated, grey buses. They neared the city and more private cars and small, working trucks appeared. Not many were new.

* * * * *

The Marianas Hotel is the best-paid accommodation in La Paz. The five-star building, surrounded outside its protected gardens by typical third-world slums, was a familiar phenomenon. Jules chose this hotel on purpose. The top echelons of Bolivian society would find the Marianas a natural watering place. Regardless of the poverty and financial hardship pervading many developing countries, outlets for excess always exist.

The car valet took the keys from Jack who handed him a twenty-dollar tip.

"I'll have it washed and ready for you in one hour, sir, okay?" the boy asked.

"Okay," replied Jack, knowing Jules had told him minutes previously they wouldn't be using the vehicle again. The Land Rover would become an unsolicited permanent addition to the Marianas car park.

The front desk handled the check-in formalities efficiently. The hotel had no such product as a regular room. Instead the travellers were installed in luxury suites. After an essential, hot bath and change of clothing they met up in Jack's suite in mid-afternoon.

"Sublime to the ridiculous, Jules, huh?" he joked.

"All for a good reason, Jack," replied Jules. He had with him the file Mac had compiled for them. "Now let's see if we can get a contact into our man."

The hotel telephone operator proved helpful. Mr Townsend's request led to an immediate connection to the main Police Headquarters in Central La Paz. Jack guessed any call coming from the Marianas merited a faster response than most.

"Hello. This is the office of the Chief of Police, Central Divisoria. How may I help you?" came a male voice.

"Good afternoon. Thank you," Jules began. "My name is Major Julian Townsend. Is it possible to speak with General Javier de Santos, please?"

"I'm so sorry, Major." The voice was all politeness. "The General isn't in the office right now. May I enquire the nature of your business with him?"

"Certainly," said Jules with his smoothest English accent. "It's a confidential matter. Should the General be in touch, would you kindly mention Major Townsend is in town, staying at the Marianas. I am interested to seek the General's assistance regarding Philip Jacoob and John Vogel. I can be reached here at the hotel." He gave him Jack's suite number.

"My pleasure, Major," the assistant replied, equally smoothly.

Jules replaced the receiver and he smiled across at Jack. "That should tickle his curiosity if nothing else."

* * * * *

The room service coffee was being delivered when the telephone rang.

Jules answered. As expected, it was the same assistant from the Chief of Police's office.

"Good afternoon again, Major. I have General de Santos on the line for you. Kindly wait a moment."

A polished voice addressed Jules.

"Good day, Major Townsend. My apologies for not getting back to you sooner. A meeting kept me tied up this afternoon."

"Good afternoon, General. Thank you for returning

my call so promptly. I understand how busy you must be, and my message to your office not being expected makes your courtesy in replying even more appreciated."

"My assistant mentioned you wish to discuss something concerning the names, Jacoob and Vogel?" enquired the General. "How may I help you?"

"Yes, indeed. A matter of some delicacy, General, which I think best discussed face to face. I'm in La Paz with a colleague of mine, Captain Jack Calder. May I be so impertinent at such short notice to ask if you're free to join us to dinner at the Marianas this evening?"

"I do have an appointment tonight already, Major, but nothing I can't postpone," came the response. "As respected visitors to Bolivia, the least I can do is to accept your gracious invitation. Say nine o'clock?"

"Nine o'clock's agreed, General. I'll reserve a private room for us. Many thanks. We'll be waiting for you in the lobby. My colleague and I look forward to meeting with you."

Jules looked pleased with the outcome of the conversation.

"If General Javier de Santos is as much of a businessman as he is a diplomat, I think we're on our way, Jack."

* * * * *

The next call was a conference link with May-Ling.

"How's the Gemtec outward shipments going?" asked Jules.

"So far everything except one shipment has gone already. No problems with any of it," she replied. "All secure this end."

"I would expect no less," said the boss. "What's the state of play with our Irishman?"

"He's doing better than expected. They moved him from the Intensive Care Unit into a private room. We still have him under heavy guard. He's complaining about that. He says give him a weapon, and he'll fend for himself," she laughed. "It'll be a couple of weeks before they release him from the hospital."

"Tie him down if you have to," added Jack. It felt good to hear her voice.

Jules then told her the missing Gemtec guys would be a problem no longer. He did not elaborate. She understood and remarked, "Fine."

CHAPTER 46

Jens Kluvin was pleased, as always, to talk with Jules.

Without preamble, Jules informed him Hubert Meiss and Nils Bergman would no longer need to be the subject of a manhunt.

"Meiss will be reported dead within a day or two when the local cops in Chile get their act together," he informed his friend. "Bergman shot him in the head while he was sleeping."

"Hmph," replied the Dutch police chief. "Justice in its own way, I suppose. Where is Bergman now?"

"Vulture fodder somewhere across the Andes, I believe. He's out of the picture too, Jens. As our friend Deryk Ostman puts it, 'Don't ask me any questions, and I won't tell you any lies.'"

"Good enough for me, Jules. Neither of their cars turned up in Europe yet. I dare say they'll surface sometime. Probably in airport carparks outside of Holland."

"What progress on the Fortune companies investigation so far?"

"Klondike time, Jules. Golden jackpot," chirped Kluvin. "May-Ling's Mr Kai's been singing like a bluebird. Plus the accounting gurus traced the payment trails and payoffs almost to a dollar.

Jules whistled appreciatively.

"We found the master files detailing the offshore structures," continued Jens. "These guys were moving drugs around Europe under cover of Gemtec's shipping arrangements. Ostman never knew a thing about it. Nils Bergman was the logistics genius. That's where his bank account money came from. Commissions and bonuses for moving cocaine in and out of anywhere you can think of in Europe."

"Cool, Jens. Shutting-down time on outlets now, I suppose?"

"You're way behind, Jules. We had a massive series of raids lasting most of the day and night yesterday. I reckon the Fortune web is well and truly cleaned out. Stacks of arrests. The cop forces are going to look good. We owe you big time on this. May-Ling was the key that opened this up for us."

"You've made our day, Jens."

"The pity is, Jules, this won't stop the drug flow," said the policeman. "A dozen more outfits like the Chans'll step up and fill the gap. At least for today, we've made a hole in their filthy business."

"Enjoy the moment, my friend. How's Donnie Mullen?"

"Mr Mullen's in seventh heaven also. A red letter week for all of us."

"Donnie's a fine cop, Jens, cut from the same block as you, I reckon."

"Jules, anytime you guys want to swap your executive salaries for a poor policeman's pay packet, give me a shout. Where are you now?"

"About to dine with one of your counterparties in La Paz, Bolivia. General Javier de Santos. You know him?"

"I was in his company once a few years back at an International Conference on Drugs in Sao Paulo, Brazil, but never got to speak with him. All the South American cop shops attended. Lots of waffle, little action. Dick de Jong sent them a flier on the Jacoob and Vogel names a couple of weeks ago. It may have reached his office, maybe not. We've had no response yet, same as with the guys in Chile. If you need any help, call me."

"Thanks Jens. Have a good day. Goodbye."

* * * * *

Jules knew Kluvin would ring Donnie Mullen soon. He beat him to the call.

Archie Campbell was finishing an update for Donnie on the various reports and concerted results of the European raids, as well as the latest developments on the triad gang front.

"Hello, stranger," Donnie began. "How are you? Where are you?"

"Jack and I are fine, Donnie, thanks. We're in South America, closing out some unfinished business."

He repeated what he'd told Jens Kluvin. The news Meiss and Bergman would no longer be a threat to anyone delighted Donnie. He already had a guilty verdict on these guys months earlier. His copper's nose for criminals had taken Donnie there a long while ago. He was pleased Jules Townsend and Jack Calder didn't have to operate under the same strictures he did.

"Jens tells me you guys scored a spectacular sweep on the drug-busting front. Magnificent."

"All positive news, Jules. As with Jens in Holland, apart from the clean-up raids, we've a stack of unassailable cases against them going back for several years, the best corporate hits we've made in years."

"Pretty comprehensive, I guess?"

"The fact the triads are scoring off each other is a huge added bonus, Jules. No-one doubts the Wong Tai Sin and Sai Kung take-downs were gangland rub-outs. In some newspapers, the Mok Kwong Cho are even publicly claiming credit for them."

"Excellent. Couldn't be better. Any hint of further triad activity against us at ISP?"

"Nothing at all, Jules. By the way, we've been keeping an eye on your Irishman. The biggest problem is persuading him he can't get out of bed yet. We're also keeping a quiet watch on May-Ling for a while.

"Much appreciated, my friend. We'll catch up soon. Cheers."

CHAPTER 47

Nine o'clock approached. Jack accompanied Jules to the lobby area of the Marianas to greet their guest. To their surprise, de Santos arrived on time. The two professional-looking bodyguards underlined the presence of a heavy-duty player.

"General de Santos. Thank you for joining us," said Jules, extending a firm handshake to the Chief of Police. "This is my partner, Captain Jack Calder."

What's with the 'Captain' all of a sudden? That was ten years and more ago.

Like his hosts, Javier de Santos was dressed in smart casual clothes. No uniform. Jack noted he bore no weapons. The bodyguards were well-armed.

"How was the traffic?" enquired Jules, leading their guest towards the ground floor private rooms.

"No problems in getting here, Major. It's a short distance from my office to the hotel."

Jules surmised an out-rider escort too, which meant the General never had an issue with traffic. Having your own private moving space in a crowded city came with the job of Chief of Police.

The trio entered the small, discreet dining salon. De Santos turned and whispered to Jules. "Major Townsend, in my business I'm obliged to be cautious at all times. In the privacy of this room will you kindly permit my attendant to…?"

"Yes of course," said Jules, not letting the General complete his question. "Understood, and perfectly in order."

He raised his arms sideways in penguin fashion. Jack followed suit. One of the bodyguards approached and body-frisked both men.

"Major Townsend, your manners are impeccable. Thank you," said the Bolivian. He nodded to the guards and they left.

To no further than outside the door. Careful man. That's why he's survived this long. Jack was impressed.

Both ISP men acknowledged the waiter serving them doubtless underwent the same body-check procedure every time he entered the salon.

An array of drinks spread across a table at the side of the room, along with two ice buckets.

Jules moved towards it. "Aperitif, General? What can I offer you?"

"I must say I do like a proper man's drink, Major. Scotch please."

"A man after my own calling," smiled Jules. "Jack? Same?"

"Sure."

Townsend poured three stiff measures and handed one to each of the other two men.

"To good company," he toasted.

"Salud!" responded their guest. He threw back the Scotch in one shot. Jules and Jack followed his example. They refilled the glasses and sat down.

The maître de took time to describe the specialties of the chef. An extensive menu also graced the table. An excellent wine list complemented each course. They ordered dinner and small talk carried them through the meal until the dessert dishes were cleared away. Business conversation was never permitted to spoil good food. The waiter poured the brandies and retired once more. Each man declined the offer of cigars.

The Police of Chief, Central Divisoria, La Paz, warmed the brandy glass in his hand before sipping.

"A superb meal, Major Townsend, Captain Calder. Splendid company into the bargain. I'm glad I postponed my other engagement tonight."

"Your presence makes it worthwhile, General. Our thanks are to you," said Jules.

"You mentioned to my assistant earlier today a couple of names you wished to discuss with me, Major?"

"Quite so. I'm not sure just how much you may be able to assist us," said the ISP boss. "I'm led to understand you are a man of considerable influence in certain matters, General. The sensitivity and delicacy of our discussion with you begs the highest possible confidentiality. I judge from your company this evening, I've no doubt you are the proper man to talk to."

"Why don't you try me, Major? These names, Jacoob and Vogel are familiar to me, but from a time some years ago, when matters in Bolivia and the border areas with Chile were, shall we say, a little problematic?"

The general refilled his brandy glass. "I checked this afternoon after our chat. I'm informed these names appeared again recently across the desk of one of my senior colleagues. A request from Amsterdam, I believe. How do you think I could help?"

"We're aware of the message sent to your colleagues," Jules replied. "My understanding is it sought information on the two persons in question. We have no such interest."

"Why?"

"Because neither Jacoob nor Vogel is alive. They both died in the last week," said Jules calmly.

Jack saw the flicker at the general's eyes. De Santos responded, "Then I wonder why you need my assistance in anything to do with two deceased persons, Major."

"That's where the delicacy arises, General."

"I suspected it might be. Please continue."

"You're aware, General, Jacoob and Vogel were aliases for two former mercenaries who peddled their services for a while in this part of the world. Hubert Meiss and Nils Bergman. They ran armed escort duties for various, shall we say, merchants? An unfortunate incident upset their masters at that time. Bergman received an injury to his leg, after which he and Meiss determined their continued health may be better guaranteed by leaving the country."

Again the flicker at the eyes. A gentle forward nod of the head.

"You're well informed, Major," said Javier de Santos. "I still am no wiser as to how I can be of assistance?"

"Over the last few years, under the alias names of Jacoob and Vogel, these men deposited a considerable sum of money in a bank here in La Paz," Jules continued. "Either man is a signatory for withdrawals on the account. The bank will not be aware of their recent deaths, nor are they ever likely to be."

Now the Chief of Police allowed himself a smile. He did not touch on the legality of what may be about to be proposed. Instead he asked, "Just how much money is involved, Major Townsend?"

"Two and a half million US dollars, General."

De Santos blinked, and reached for a small piece of dessert chocolate close to his brandy glass. They had his attention, and his interest. He took several more moments chewing the chocolate before posing his next question.

"And how is that sum to be made accessible, which I assume is your objective, without proper legal signatures? A perfectly reasonable question, don't you think, Major? Captain?" His smile was friendly, but his eyes narrowed as he looked across at his hosts.

Jules now understood the General wasn't considering whether he should assist to access the money, but how.

"Copies of these signatures are available as we speak, General. The hypothetical question remains, do you believe it feasible to assist in the delicacy of extracting it from Banco Credito Primera, where it currently sits? With no living ownership?"

"Speaking hypothetically, my dear Major Townsend, I've found most things are feasible. In any such matter, it comes down to how much persuasion is required and in what circumstances. For discussion purposes only you understand, how much persuasion is available?"

Without hesitation, Jules replied. "One million dollars."

The general smiled again. "That's a lot of persuasion, my friend. And the other one point five million dollars?"

"To be remitted by wire transfer to a named bank in the Channel Islands."

"All of this is very interesting, Major." Jules knew the police chief was totally in command of what would happen next.

Will he bite or not?

"Tonight is the first time we've had the pleasure of meeting," he continued. "Your company has been charming and our discussion most interesting. I've enjoyed it immensely. Tell me this, however. If such an operation were to be undertaken, how would you be comfortable some third party wouldn't arrange to secure all of the money for themselves?"

Some third party like General Javier de Santos himself, and cutting us out of it. Jack knew they'd reached the 'shit or get off the pot' time.

Jules responded. "Whoever may feel inclined to assist in this venture will know how grateful my associates will be for any help given."

"We all have associates, Major," replied de Santos. "Which are you referring to?"

Jules began to unbutton the left-hand sleeve of his shirt and nodded to Jack to do likewise.

The Bolivian watched them with a quizzical look.

They rolled up their sleeves to uncover a tattoo on each of their left forearms. About three inches long, their tattoos displaying the winged dagger across the open blade of which the banner read 'Who Dares Wins' met the General's eyes. The unmistakable crest and insignia of the SAS.

Javier de Santos was impressed. "Major Townsend, Captain Calder, I salute your most powerful of credentials. I would be honoured to work with you to find a satisfactory conclusion in all of this. Now you mentioned something about signatures?"

CHAPTER 48

They didn't doubt their suites had been searched while dining with de Santos. That was expected. The tell-tale removal of a single hair from certain drawer areas and door jambs told its own story. The searchers were unaware of the anonymous box given earlier in the evening to the luggage clerk to retain for Mr Calder until the morning. The plain, cardboard box contained the silencers, the pistols, and the daggers.

Detail, detail, detail.

De Santos sat in the middle sofa while Jules fetched the slim package from his papers. These documents would mean nothing to the search party. He handed a copy of the Jacoob and Vogel signatures to the police chief.

"The images have been enhanced, General." said Jules. "They should be sufficient for use?"

De Santos inspected the signatures of Philip Jacoob and John Vogel. He nodded approval.

"Acquired from where, Major?"

"My associates, General," Jules replied. "Our networks extend to most parts of the world. Information on people such as Meiss and Bergman is common currency in our business."

"I must confess that's far better organized than the authorities I work with in South America."

"On this sheet are the details of the Channel Islands bank account." said Jules. "One and a half million dollars to be remitted there. As for the balance, I have no interest at all. Do we have a deal?"

General de Santos rose to his feet. He extended his hand first to Jules and then to Jack. "Gentlemen, we have a deal."

"Good. Let's drink to that," replied Jules.

"If you wouldn't mind, Major, I think I've had my quota for the evening. I'd prefer a clear head in the morning to address our situation. I'll contact you toward the middle of the afternoon tomorrow. Okay with you?"

The Bolivian made his way to the door. Jack opened it for their guest and the two bodyguards outside the suite stepped to either side ready to escort their boss from the premises.

When de Santos had gone Jack said, "Remind me never to play poker with you, Jules."

Jules laughed in the relaxed way he always did when an operation went without problems. He reached for the Scotch bottle.

"Let's enjoy a real drink. We're not doing anything until at least midday tomorrow by the sound of things."

"How did you know he'd play ball?"

"I didn't know for sure. You can't tell which way these guys'll jump. In parts of Africa, say, or some other places with no semblance of law and order it wouldn't work. They'd take the lot and slice our throats. General Javier has built a structure here over several years. He won't risk having it threatened. Our affiliation with the SAS tells him we've got friends who'd come looking for him if he screwed us up. Even if he thought we're no longer in the regiment he'd probably respect us. This guy's a survivor. He's been around for what, thirty years in this game? His lifestyle tells you he's no angel. For sure he looks after a lot of rice bowls one way or another. Remember the training, Jack? When you're in the jungle, use the jungle, don't fight it, right?"

"Right," agreed Jack, pouring another Scotch. "Cheers."

* * * * *

Jules Townsend's assessment of the Chief of Police, Central Divisoria, La Paz, Javier de Santos, wasn't far off the mark.

His car emerged from the Marianas driveway and de Santos let his shoulders relax back into the rear seat's ample leather, his mind focused. In his mid-fifties now, the young man who started as a trainee legal intern in the government's law offices more than thirty years earlier had seen profound changes from the direction his career path initially signalled so long ago.

He remembered the impoverished family background in which both of his parents died during his early teens. The local school headmaster recognized his deep measure of intelligence and nurtured the boy's thinking talents. With some persuasion he secured the support of his own brother, a Congressman in La Paz, to get the lad into an apprenticeship in the administration's training programmes. His agile brain and quick grasp of legal process led to a rapid rise through the offices of various influential politicians.

Early in that era of dog eat dog, Javier realized remaining within the bar profession had limited upside. Time and again he observed the ease with which the law became subverted to the whims of those appointed to uphold it. He made a conscious decision in his early twenties to join the ranks of the police force, his intent to secure the position of ranking officer by the time he reached thirty. He beat his deadline by a year and a half. Running regional forces up and down the border gave him an even deeper realization life was patently unfair. There was none of the equality the early law courses espoused. However, he also came to terms with the fact he was not cut out for the role of a crusader.

His intermediation skills with local and regional politicians served him in good stead as the various business cartels overlapped with the drug-running businesses. He managed to remain on the fringes of the gang warfare erupting in the townships and rural areas dividing Chile and Bolivia. His reputation developed as a police commander who got things done without upsetting too many people. It was a delicate skill.

Ultimate promotion to General and one of six regional Chiefs of Police by the age of forty meant he choose his own jurisdiction. Long-term seniority was not widespread in the Bolivian police force. He settled on the Central Divisoria in La Paz. Serious crime could be tackled in the city without causing waves among the big fish. Success as measured by arrests was easier in La Paz.

Javier de Santos was under no illusion. It could all change overnight. He took care to secrete away enough invisible wealth to protect his retirement, which he hoped would not be too far in the future.

The meeting with Major Julian Townsend and Captain Jack Calder provided the ideal opportunity for the final impetus towards that retirement date. In the morning he would make an appointment with an old acquaintance, Alfredo Suarez. Suarez pulled all the strings at Banco Credito Primera in La Paz these days.

CHAPTER 49

A request to meet with the Chief of Police is not a regular entry in the diaries of bank General Managers. With some bemusement, Alfredo Suarez agreed to lunch with General Javier de Santos. The prestigious Bankers Club in the centre of town provided one of the few benefits available in a profession sadly lacking in attraction in a battered economy.

Suarez had met professionally with de Santos many times before in the course of his ten-year tenure as the head of Banco Credito Primera's operations in La Paz. The frequent cocktail parties and diplomatic call-overs provided occasional glamour and further excuse for free entertainment. Very little real business ever transacted at these events. The need to see and be seen was part of the financial community's fragile hold on the Bolivian economy.

Suarez's respected standing in the community consisted more of perception than reality. Most businessmen who survived longer than a decade had some skeletons in their closets. No angels operated commercially in La Paz.

Part of General Javier de Santos's own survival skills included awareness of these histories.

The smartly-dressed banker shook hands with the Chief of Police as they sat down at their corner table. The tables in the club positioned far enough apart to ensure privacy of conversation. The obvious glances from other diners in the room were part of the ritual. See and be seen. The usual cross-sections of the capital's business elite scattered through the restaurant, the pantomime of meeting commercial peers enough to guarantee a full dining room daily at the Bankers Club. Suarez contemplated his companion's agenda today.

As with dinner, so with lunch, no business matters discussed until coffee arrived. This was South America.

They shared only one bottle of wine, a concession to a lunchtime engagement. A decent cognac along with the espressos lent some balance to the palate.

"Alfredo, it's been a while since we had time together like this. We should be doing this more often," began de Santos, leaning back in order to sweep the room with his eyes.

"I'm thinking the same thing, Javier. Too much business, not enough time for friends," he replied.

"How's the family? Your wife Marta? Your daughter Emilia?"

"Both well. Marta's cancer's in remission, thanks be to God. Emilia was accepted at the University of La Paz this year. We have high hopes for her."

"The little bit of nonsense with your daughter all resolved now?"

"Yes. Your intervention in that misunderstanding is much appreciated, my dear Javier."

Like most of her social contemporaries, his only child, Emilia Suarez, had dabbled with cocaine in her late teens. On a crazy, summer evening, one of her succession of drug-fuelled lovers had shot dead a customer in a downtown nightclub. When the police arrests were made, Emilia had been slumped senseless on a table beside her boyfriend. Javier de Santos had intervened after desperate pleading from Alfredo Suarez. De Santos realized the girl had nothing to do with the shooting. She recognized the event as a wake-up call. Three months in a drug rehabilitation centre had worked wonders for her.

"I'm glad to hear she's doing well, Alfredo," the policeman nodded. "She's a good kid. With your Marta's illness, you don't need any distractions to get you derailed, huh?"

"Quite so." Suarez wondered where this was leading.

"How are things at the bank?"

"Slow to be honest, but we make enough to keep the shareholders happy. These are tough times, Javier."

"You still look after the main business, right?"

"Well, I don't do it all on my own, Javier," laughed Suarez. "I have dozens of people who do what I tell them."

Precisely why de Santos was dining with him today.

"Alfredo. A situation has developed which may be of some interest to you, given the fortunate position you hold."

Now we're getting to it.

"Tell me. What's on your mind? I didn't think we're here just to test the wine list."

"It seems a couple of criminals, foreigners, have been using the bank to launder a considerable amount of money. Perhaps over several years, but certainly a large sum in the last two or three weeks."

"Oh? You have details on this? I'll check immediately and get back to you. I'll find the account and put a stop on it today."

"On the contrary. No need to do either of these things, my dear friend," the policeman said, with a smile on his face. "I know already the account name and number. Also, I have no wish to stop transactions. Quite the opposite in fact."

"Enlighten me, please," asked Alfredo, cautiously.

Javier pushed two folded sheets across the table to his dining partner.

"These men are no longer alive. The names are aliases, therefore there will never be a trace they existed. The signatures on the second sheet reflect what you have in the bank's records. There will be no claimants on the account. It would be a pity to see it go to waste."

The banker scrutinized the sheets carefully.

De Santos continued in a quiet voice. No risk of being overheard from any of the adjacent tables. "I would suggest through your good graces this be handled quite invisibly, my dear Alfredo. For you to make the transfers listed at the lower half of the first sheet I give you my word you will receive cash of one hundred thousand dollars. I think such a sum will go a long way to helping with the expense of caring for our dear Marta. It should also ensure Emilia's university education continues unbroken."

The policeman sat back in his chair and called for another cognac for each of them.

He watched for the response from the banker, knowing his companion's mind was busy working out the chances of discovery. He also knew having the proposition put to him by the Chief of Police, turning down the request would probably be by far the worse course of action. One hundred thousand dollars amounted to more money than he could earn even up through the end of his career. He had domestic financial pressures to deal with. The two most important people in his life needed caring for, albeit in different ways. His record at the bank was exemplary. His instructions in the line of business would never be under question. The decision was simple.

"You say these men are dead, Javier?"

"I promise you. No comebacks. Ever."

"When do you wish this completed?"

"Today's as good a day as any, don't you think?"

"Consider it done."

The men shook hands. For each, this had been a most profitable lunch.

* * * * *

Later in the evening, Javier de Santos met with Jack and Jules in the latter's suite.

He handed an envelope to Jules and said, "Details of the transfer as agreed, Major Townsend. Executed today. I'd be grateful if you will call your bank in the Channel Islands to confirm receipt before you leave La Paz. I'm sure you approach business as I do. I don't like loose ends."

Jules thanked him and opened the envelope. A flimsy pink piece of paper protruded which Jules read. Jack caught the raising of an eyebrow from his partner.

"This transfer amount is for one million, six hundred and fifty thousand dollars, General. I only expected one million five hundred thousand?" queried Jules.

"Major Townsend, the account already had funds of a further one hundred and fifty thousand from payments made into the bank several years ago," explained de Santos. "We agreed persuasion expenses at only one million dollars. A deal is a deal, my friend. The account is now closed."

Jules laughed and extended his hand to de Santos.

"General, Captain Calder and I will be delighted to host you to dinner in Europe one day soon. Thank you."

With a nod of the head and a smile, the Bolivian left the ISP men still shaking their heads.

Honour sometimes comes in strange packages.

CHAPTER 50

Over a month had passed since their return from South America during which time Jack and his boss were busier than ever with ISP. The monthly security operations review in Amsterdam with Peter Dewer had just finished. Word of the successful protective operation in Hong Kong had percolated the Dutch market. A flood of enquiries had been received from other centres across Europe. Success breeds success. Extra hiring programs were in full swing to maintain the flow of business needed to prosper without any lowering of the high standards demanded by the boss.

They met with Deryk Ostman as usual in the owner's office. The Gemtec man discussed with them the creation of a fund to assist employees and their families from the security industry who suffered injury or death in the execution of their duties.

Ostman supported the plan with ISP from the outset. He had persuasive influence with the chief executives of all of the major companies affiliated to the Gems and Jewellers Association across Holland. Not one resisted the idea. Initial thoughts centred around a modest percentage of annual profits being managed by professional money managers, reporting to a committee of the companies represented.

Deryk Ostman, together with Jack Calder and Jules Townsend met with the families of the courier and the escort shot down by the robbers in Utrecht. Each family received a bank draft for half a million dollars. This was not intended to replace their killed loved ones. It was hoped it would go a long way to alleviating any financial hardship caused by their loss.

A balance of one hundred and fifty thousand dollars from an account in the Channel Islands became the seed money for the fund.

* * * * *

Annie Bell returned to Poole in Dorset soon after her husband Roddie's shooting at the Rotterdam warehouse. Her daughter and young family lived a few houses away in the same street.

Ostman flew across to England to join Jules and Jack on that visit. The three of them journeyed together in a hired limousine through the southern countryside, enjoying some of the best scenery England has to offer on the way to Dorset. Annie Bell's house sat in a row of older, semi-detached, red-brick houses perched on a raised part of the town, overlooking the sea. The widow waited at the door as they pulled up outside. Jules and Jack both hugged her close. She was part of their family too. Deryk Ostman shook hands in his proper, gentlemanly, Dutch style.

The pain still etched across her face as she sat with them in her front lounge, her daughter on the couch beside her. Tea and scones were more than adequate for her visitors. In typical English manner, conversation centred on small talk, the weather, and the journey down to Dorset.

Words relating to her Roddie were not needed. Annie Bell had understood a long time ago her husband had chosen a career which inevitably would risk putting him in the line of fire. She just didn't expect it to continue after he left the SAS.

Jules explained what the envelope contained. In Annie Bell's life, she couldn't contemplate that kind of money. It was a king's ransom to her.

"You're good men, all of you. Jules, Jack, Mr Ostman. My family and I are grateful for your kindness. I thank God I've got my daughter and grandkids. But I still miss my Roddie."

She started to weep quietly as her daughter held her hand, and then put her arm around her mother's shoulders.

The visitors rose to go. Mrs Bell nudged the tears away from her eyes and came forward to each man in turn and hugged them tightly, this time including Deryk Ostman.

Jack Calder was now more than ever convinced the operations they'd undertaken in Hong Kong and Chile were totally justified. He often considered the legal system devoid of the means of balancing justice properly.

Annie Bell and her dignity testified to that.

CHAPTER 51

It was a busy three years following the gem heists in Holland and the attack in Hong Kong. The ISP group operations now covered most of Europe. Guardwell was acquired in Holland to add to ISP's capabilities across the continent.

Morg Landis, ex-Guardwell boss, became firmly installed as a full partner in that division of the company, looking after the Low Countries operations. Peter Dewer fulfilled his early promise and ran the pan-European business, based in London. The re-uniting of former Guardwell colleagues, Landis and Dewer was a master stroke. The partnership bred significant growth in new accounts.

In Hong Kong, DCI Donnie Mullen took early retirement from the Royal Hong Kong Police Force a year ahead of the nineteen ninety-seven hand-over to mainland China. He readily accepted the offer from Jules Townsend to take over the management of the Asian countries businesses for ISP.

In Amsterdam, Jens Kluvin continued to repel the overtures from Jules to come join the group at Advisory Board level. He maintained he still had a few years more left in him yet before he surrendered his policeman's badge. The promise to consider the offer, however, would stay on his desk. Jules expected that would be at least another five years away. The big Dutchman enjoyed the action in his current position too much to leave.

Jack Calder and Malky McGuire had been made full equal partners in the group a year earlier. Jules reckoned their grasp of the broader requirements of ISP had reached the level he and the business required of them.

* * * * *

The Crushed Grapes Bar in Soho had changed little in the intervening three years. It still provided excellent Scotch, although the hammerings it received from Jack and Malky were fewer now than before.

They were enjoying a couple of early evening glasses before the pre-dinner rush to round off a good day in the office. Another large account that morning had agreed to move to ISP. A little celebration was in order.

They finished the second drink and Jack asked his buddy, "You got any change for the phone?"

Automatically, the Irishman stuck his hand in his pocket and displayed a few coins to his partner.

Then he said, "Who you calling?"

Jack chuckled, taking the money from him, "Much as I could stay here and get wasted with you, big man, I'm just gonna call May-Ling to tell her I'm coming home shortly. I don't want to miss putting wee Tommy to bed. I can't miss tucking in my son two nights in a row, now can I?"

Seumas Gallacher enjoys being in touch with his readers. You are invited to interact with him on the social networking circuit as follows:

Blog   : seumasgallacher.com

Facebook : www.facebook.com/seumasgallacher

Twitter   : @seumasgallacher

Email   : seumasgallacher@yahoo.com